TOUGH
SCRATCHES

TOUGH SCRATCHES

Finding the Path BOOK 2

Eichin Chang-Lim

TATE PUBLISHING
AND **ENTERPRISES, LLC**

Published by Tate Publishing & Enterprises, LLC
127 E. Trade Center Terrace | Mustang, Oklahoma 73064 USA
1.888.361.9473 | www.tatepublishing.com

Tate Publishing is committed to excellence in the publishing industry. The company reflects the philosophy established by the founders, based on Psalm 68:11,
"The Lord gave the word and great was the company of those who published it."

Book design copyright © 2014 by Tate Publishing, LLC. All rights reserved.
Cover design by Rodrigo Adolfo
Interior design by Mary Jean Archival

Published in the United States of America

ISBN: 978-1-62902-429-5
1. Fiction / General
2. Fiction / Romance / Contemporary
13.11.20

DEDICATION

To all the people who constantly have to gather up their dwindling strength and cling tight to their dreams and goals through life's ups and downs.

CONTENTS

CHAPTER 1

REALITY! HOW CRUEL!

Kayla felt lightheaded. She jumped out of the chair and headed to the exit door; Dr. Leon quickly followed. Kayla could not recall the last time she went to a bar.

Stopping in her tracks, she realized they were inconveniently standing by the glass swivel doors of the bar. "Let's discuss this outside," Kayla had told the irresistible (and sweet *and* intelligent) Dr. Leon. She knew she had to confess her blunders. She knew that spending time with him was dangerous. Especially *this* kind of time. Especially for a married woman.

Kayla had met her husband in high school during her junior year during a beach cleanup with her best friend, Breeana. They became serious quickly, and Kayla became pregnant the summer before her senior year. In spite of the difficulties, she had the baby, and she and Russell kept their relationship going strongly. Because money was an issue, and Russell wanted to propose to Kayla, he delivered a box for his friend in hopes of gaining extra cash. He took it to the correct location and awaited the extra money.

But that box had drugs and weapons in it.

Russell was sent to jail. In order to gain the rights of a "private visit," Kayla boldly decided to marry Russell while he was in jail, before the trial.

During the trial, the jury wasn't in his favor; he was sentenced to seven years in a prison in South Dakota. From that point on, she struggled as a single mother trying also to pursue her education and distract herself from the pain of separation from her husband.

Because Kayla was pursuing her nursing degree, she was required to complete a hospital externship before she could graduate. There she met the ER doctor who was charming her now.

Earlier that night, they were sitting at the bar inside, dimly lit aside from blue light shining through the glassy bar that illuminated their drinks. It was a scene with the typical Friday night crowd. Thankfully they were sitting side by side, like two chums discussing the day's hard work. Their position allowed Kayla to avert her eyes as she absentmindedly stirred her Peach Melba cooler. Her heart raced as he spoke.

"I've always liked you, Kayla," he said. He smiled like he was grateful she would agree to come out with him—and he thanked her numerous times! Kayla groaned thinking about how humble he was. His kind eyes shone behind his black-rimmed glasses.

"I…like hanging out with you, too," she said. Her stomach muscles clenched from the impact of her words. The quick tempo of the bar's bass-heavy music beat in time with her pounding heart.

Dr. Leon rested his cheek on his hand and turned toward her. "It's taken a long time for us to find mutual free time. Maybe we can hang out more often?"

Kayla chomped down on her lips as if trying to hold back words she knew she shouldn't utter. She had an itching for Dr. Leon but also knew she wasn't going to be *that* type of wife.

What am I doing?

Kayla simply smiled. No harm done, no words she would regret.

But then Dr. Leon agreed to nonverbal communication, too. His hands, rough from continuously washing his hands at the hospital, swept aside a wisp of Kayla's bangs and gently nestled it behind her ear.

Red flag. Get out of here.

"Excuse me. I have to go," Kayla said, already standing up and pushing the bar stool under the table.

"Kayla…what?"

She could hear Dr. Leon pursuing her as she took longer strides toward the door. He still caught up with her as the mildly crisp, cool Northern California air greeted her outside. She realized that it was time to get the truth out.

"Remember when I mentioned making trips to South Dakota? Do you know why?" she asked breathlessly.

He just looked straight at her without a word. Kayla continued,

"I went to visit my husband. He is my daughter's father and is incarcerated there."

Dr. Leon was obviously shocked but furrowed his brow, as if trying to make all efforts to focus on Kayla's words and their implications. She could almost hear his brain ticking in analysis.

Slowly, he exhaled before taking in another deep breath. "Kayla, it may sound insane, but if I don't say it now, it may haunt me for the rest of my life. I have been attracted to you since I first saw you. I'm drawn to you for some reason. It's your personality…you make me so happy whenever you're around. I thought we had some kind of connection, you know? I was wondering why you were trying so hard to avoid me. You even seemed to like me. Well, it all makes sense now." He paused, leaving a heavy silence hanging in the air. "Sorry, I don't mean to sound cheesy."

As Kayla listened with shifting eyes, Dr. Leon continued in a soft, pleading voice. "Kayla, all I want now is a friendly hug before we say good-bye."

Their eyes locked as Dr. Leon drew her in slowly. She could feel his passion welling within him, but he exercised reserve. As her head lay against his chest, she could hear his quickened heartbeat. Gently, Dr. Leon broke away from her. No doubt years of emergency room training conditioned him to use his brain in overriding his emotions when unexpected circumstances arose.

"Kayla, let me walk you to the bus station."

Appreciating the gesture, especially at that time of night, Kayla gave him a small smile.

As they walked the two blocks, it was mostly silent until Kayla heard Dr. Leon muttering to himself. "It's pathetic… whoever said 'love is not possessive'?"

Moments later, he said, "It's cruel to desire something that does not belong to me…"

Kayla felt helpless. "I'm so sorry."

"It's not your fault," Dr. Leon cut in. "It's something I need to deal with myself."

Determined not to make anything complicated, Kayla kept her feelings and thoughts to herself. *I should just play it cool*, she reminded herself. As he said, she needed to deal with it herself, too. She had her own share of pains and frustrations, but verbalizing it was not an option at the moment.

It was silent aside from their shoes hitting the pavement during their uncomfortable walk. Kayla was relieved to see the dark silhouette of the bus station bench. As she walked toward the curb, hugging herself in her cardigan, Dr. Leon stepped back and leaned against the brick wall. During minutes that felt like hours, the bus finally rumbled down the quiet road and stopped.

Kayla glanced behind her as she stepped up into the bus. In an almost inaudible whisper, Kayla heard Dr. Leon's words. "Please take care, Kayla…"

In the reflection of the streetlight (or was it Kayla's imagination?) she could see tears in his eyes. She quickly boarded and slumped into a seat. As the bus moved slowly onward, she couldn't help but glance back once more. Dr. Leon was still leaning against the wall without movement. He was like a statue.

It takes a lot of courage and honesty for a man like him to share his vulnerability with me, Kayla thought sadly. To honor that, she vowed to keep the night's encounter between only them.

As Kayla unlocked the trailer door, she was alone. Veronica kept Alexis over night for Joycelyn's birthday. She fell back into her normal resolute mindset. Alexis's book bag lay on the floor, along with her dirty sneakers.

"Yes. This is my reality, my duty, and my responsibility... my daughter and her father."

As if on cue, Russell's letters to her – now brighter, hopeful, and romantic once again rather than self-loathing – reeled her back in. She knew she loved him. He was worth the wait.

Kayla passed the beautiful, springy afternoon with Dorothy, who was wearing a lavender handkerchief that day. They were reclining on the top step of her porch and crossing their legs on the bottom two. Kayla looked off at the tall, uncut grass behind the wire fence around the park. The image of Dr. Leon was redolent in her mind, but she remembered her promise to herself. She turned to a cheerful topic instead.

"Oh, I forgot to tell you – I'm done with my program now," said Kayla, fist-pumping the air. "I just need to pass the State Board License Exam for RN. That's getting difficult with the upcoming date..."

"Why you talking to me, then? Go study. You have that light at the end of the tunnel." Dorothy waved her orange, sparkly-nailed hand toward Kayla's door. Kayla agreed.

However, when she began studying, she just couldn't. Tapping her pencil against the table, Kayla daydreamed, eyes drifting off her workbook.

*We'll actually be able to hug, kiss, sleep together…*Kayla thought she would be in sensation overload. Russell was like a distant memory of a sweet dream. She couldn't believe it had been seven years. Wrought with pain, those years were also full of her logistics planning for each step. She was so busy that she managed to keep herself numb to the pain – most of the time. Powered by each trip to Russell, she let that be her navigator instead of the distant date he would be released.

But what if those visits were only enjoyable because of their scarcity? What if their situation was like Christmas – where people enjoy time with their raucous extended family, simply because they see them so infrequently and it's only one short day?

The thought immobilized Kayla.

Unsurprisingly, Kayla failed her State Board Exam the first time. She studied her feelings, not the books. Her outrage was great, but she knew she had to buckle down this time. She felt like she not only let herself down, but also her family. She tried to shake the word *failure* from her mind.

"Alexis, once I pass this test, I'm a free woman again," she said to her ten-year-old as they sat at the table. Both had their books out, though Kayla's was about as thick as the Bible. *And soon after, Daddy will be back…*

"It's fine," said Alexis with a shrug. She did her own math homework beside Kayla. Fractions weren't her strong suit, and she had four pages full of them. The way she furrowed brow as she worked, her tongue slightly sticking out, reminded Kayla of Russell's habit. Whenever she saw Alexis do that, she felt guilty – like a piece of Russell was monitoring her.

"You can't beat yourself up over Dr. Dreamboat forever," said Dorothy with her hands on her hips. "It's only natural – you've been alone for so many years!"

"Ugh. I guess I'm freaking out about what could've been," Kayla replied. Then, with a rueful smile, "And the inappropriate dreams."

"Oh Kay, you're nasty." Dorothy playfully hit her arm.

As Kayla's anxiety rose about reuniting with Russell, she wrote to him about her day. He was essentially her diary. By contrast, he was short –

Dear Kayla,

I'm so sorry to hear you didn't pass. But hey, think about Thomas Edison. It took him, what, hundreds of tries to get the light bulb?

Kayla rolled her eyes. *He was an inventor. Not the same thing. I'm not that noble.*

I know you're probably thinking, "He was an inventor, dummy. I'm just trying to pass a test other nurses have to take." Still though, same idea applies. Successes don't happen overnight. I love you, and I'm proud you've come so far from that girl wondering how she'd go to college.

Tell Alexis I miss her. Make sure she aces that math test.

S.O.S: Same Old Stuff on my end (as I always begin my letters). I'm reading a lot of books lately. Just finished some Kurt Vonnegut. What do you recommend?

I love you so much. I can't believe I see you soon. Time is going even slower the closer we get.

Love, Russell

Kayla closed her eyes and slumped back in the tall-backed wooden chair at the table.

How could she have thought about cheating?

She marked another day off of the calendar. Russell would be back home so soon. She could barely breathe at the thought.

Kayla failed a second time.

Feeling deeply depressed and defeated, she wondered how to healthily cope with the stress that was now smothering her. After all her hard work toward her future, she couldn't give up. She had a daughter to think of and soon, a husband, home again.

At the health club, she swiped lawyers and business people's cards and saw them transition from their stiff suits to loose-fitting basketball shorts and t-shirts. With that, they jumped on cardio machines and appeared to desperately run away from their day and its pressures.

Now there's an idea, Kayla thought. Because she worked at the health club, she was entitled to use the workout equipment for free as part of her employment benefits. It was time to get in shape.

After tossing flats and sandals out of her closet, Kayla found old running shoes and set off for the club. She tried not to feel intimidated as she walked in, but having worked there for so long, she had seen *all* types of people use the amenities. Feeling alien on the treadmill, she placed her hands on the side and started off at a leisurely pace. By the end of a forty-five-minute session, she was sprinting on the treadmill, sweating out her feelings, unable to think about anything except her gasping breath. Her physical exhaustion blocked any unwelcome thoughts from her mind. It only improved after she wiped the sweat from her brow and threw off her damp shirt. After the endorphins came her focus and concentration.

To add to that, her family had her covered.

"That's it," said Veronica, after hearing the news from Alexis. "I'm back to offering casseroles and childcare services."

"I couldn't ask you to do that…well, okay, yes. Yes I could," said Kayla with a grin.

"Glad to see you've come around so quickly. I'll call Mrs. Mancini to make sure she can help when needed."

"Shucks, sister. You're not so bad after all," joked Kayla.

That night, she made a pot of coffee. Her distress at not passing twice made it so she had no choice but to focus on the test. Third time is the charm, she thought.

With dedication, plenty of late nights, and help from the increasingly excited Mrs. Mancini as well as Veronica, Kayla passed the next test. She could finally breathe easily – the first and second failure had stolen her breath for a good, long while.

CHAPTER 2

REUNITED

"Are you nervous?" said Dorothy as Kayla flitted to and fro in her trailer. "You're like a distressed turkey the day before Thanksgiving. Relax and imagine how great it will be."

"Let's hope," said Kayla, breathing deeply.

It was the long-awaited day. It was surreal; they couldn't wrap their minds around it after the grueling years apart. Kayla spent so many nights curled up with a pillow dwelling on the concept of time – all the minutes that turned into hours that dripped by. The days accumulated into years achingly slow when she thought of it in terms of Russell's incarceration.

Kayla had to give Alexis a serious talk about how her father would be living with them now. She mentioned it now and again, but Alexis has awaited it for so long that it felt like a day that would never come. Now that it was, they had to discuss the possibilities.

"Your father loves you, no matter how he reacts to the real world. It's been a long time since he's been in it," warned Kayla. "But what are you thinking about? How are you doing?"

She combed her fingers through her daughter's hair as Alexis looked down at her worn sneakers. They sat on the pink quilt of her bed that the stuffed animals protected under their unblinking gaze.

"I don't know. It's just weird I guess. It's permanent now."

"There's nothing to be worried about. Your father has been waiting to see you for ages."

After some quiet moments, Alexis stared at her mom. Now resembling her mother, she had messy brown hair that was always halfheartedly scooped in a ponytail, or loose strands fell out from playing soccer at school. But she had Russell's otherworldly, oceanic eyes. They penetrated Kayla as she spoke, windows of emotion.

"You would never tell me why Dad ended up there. Did he…do anything bad? Like…hurting somebody?"

Kayla's stomach went numb and her heart went out to her daughter. She felt like a rotten mother. "I'm so sorry that I haven't reassured you of this before. No, your father isn't violent. He shouldn't even be where he is."

"I know, you always said that."

"He…wanted to propose to me. Ask me to marry him. And he went about it the wrong way."

"How?"

Kayla closed her eyes and wondered how to describe the concept of "drugs" to a young girl. "Basically, someone tricked him and gave him stuff to sell that *wasn't* his to sell. A cop caught him. That's all we need to know. That's really it."

Alexis looked suspicious but loosened up. They hugged for a prolonged period of time, Kayla stroking her hair. And then she looked at the clock.

"Time to go to the airport." She smiled. "I've been waiting to say that for years."

Mrs. Mancini bounced around, her instability rivaling Kayla's ("And I didn't think it possible," Kayla muttered with a smile). Veronica came solo, often putting her arms around Alexis protectively. After watching her so often, she and Mrs. Mancini were like Alexis's other mothers. Kayla's jaw was set with determination to change that and to be significantly available for her daughter now that she had Russell back and wasn't juggling school with work. But at that moment, she wasn't thinking of it. She paced around the airport nervously.

"I should've worn more deodorant," she told Alexis with a goofy grin, trying to lighten her mood. "I'm so excited. Is my shirt soaked? My palms are definitely sweaty."

She playfully put her palms against Alexis's shirt as she wrinkled her nose. "That's so gross. Stop it, Mom."

Earlier that morning, Russell signed the paperwork mechanically. Upon Russell's completion, the security guard brusquely set a gray sweatshirt on the table, ushering him to follow him to freedom.

Freedom…

A concept previously so elusive was now his to grab. But with it came the fact he was starting from scratch. Freedom felt foreign. Scary, even.

Russell walked out the gate feeling like he was walking for the first time, expecting to fall.

Normally prisoners were released by bus. Thanks to his parents and Kayla's joint effort, they managed to buy him a plane ticket. They didn't want to wait a second longer to see him.

"Is that him?" said Veronica, squinting at the shape from far away.

Kayla couldn't swallow as Mrs. Mancini recited, "Oh my God, oh my God." Freezing, they saw it was only a doppelganger. They all decompressed and continued scoping out every person that exited the gate.

"We need to coordinate logistics," said Kayla. "Veronica, walk over to the left – near the vending machine. I'll go to my right. You guys stay here." With so many people exiting, they spread out in hopes of citing him immediately.

Kayla's heart beat so fast she thought it would give out. She felt like she was running a marathon. "So," she asked Alexis for distraction, ignoring her dry mouth. "Do you remember what he looks like?"

Alexis's watery eyes fixed on a distant point. She nodded solemnly before turning up to face Kayla. "Yeah, I do."

"Good."

"It's him." Alexis calmly pointed to the tall, thin man ahead of them.

"Oh my God!" shrieked Mrs. Mancini. She clung to her purse and darted over to Alexis and Kayla. "It's him!"

There he was. The sight of her husband, finally free. His shoulders were hunched over, like his carry-on bag was much heavier than it was. Except there was no carry-on bag. He had a clear five o'clock shadow. Even within the last year, Russell looked older. Like the last year of prison left the roughest mark on him.

When Russell was finally approaching them, everyone shot up and started cheering like he was a celebrity. His mother was bawling; Kayla had definite streams of tears rolling down her face. Alexis couldn't contain her contagious smiles. Even Veronica, who had told Kayla multiple times that maybe marriage wasn't the best option, was cheering.

Russell gave a bashful smile and looked like he didn't know what to do with himself. His limbs hung awkwardly like he was a chimp in the airport. Kayla didn't have time to think of this. She bolted, tackled him, and squeezed him with all her might. She even wrapped a leg around him too, standing on the toes of her left foot. Russell laughed. Not as muscled as Kayla remembered; he was thinner. But the strength of his embrace suggested otherwise.

"I can't believe it, I can't believe it," murmured Kayla, buried in Russell's shirt. A few tears escaped his eyes and trickled down to her brown head. "You should've escaped sooner, through the sewers," said Kayla with a laugh, referencing *The Shawshank Redemption*.

Mrs. Mancini soon followed, kissing Russell and putting her arm around both him and Kayla. After being reunited, then Russell laid eyes on Alexis. Everyone stood aside.

"Can I have a hug?" he asked.

Alexis gave a crooked smile and ran up to him, hugging him with all her might. Maybe she'd have been nervous otherwise, but at seeing everyone else's public displays of intense affection, she followed suit. Russell didn't want to let go of her – finally with his girl, finally able to know her.

◆—→

"I can't believe it. You're here."

Kayla and Russell lay in bed together, listening to the constant hum of the table fan rotating back and forth. Kayla's head was in the crook of Russell's arm as they stare at the ceiling. Running her fingers along the soft underside of his arm, she thought she was dreaming. Soon she'd wake up in the same bed and find herself alone, as she had for roughly the past 2,560 days. She glanced back up at him and saw him in dusk's purple-orange light filtering through the blinds.

"You can't stop smiling," he said.

"Neither can you."

Kayla gently turned over to better look at him. His face was certainly more careworn for his almost twenty-nine years of age. He looked more thoughtful, somehow. Hopefully thinking of her.

"Now we're stuck together," she said with a teasing smile. "Whether you like it or not. Back to 'the ol' ball and chain.'"

Kayla expected his old sarcasm, something like, "I could think of nothing worse." When he didn't even smile, she realized he was figuratively held down for the past seven years.

Her ears burned. Before she had time to open her mouth again, Russell leaned over, placed his hands on both sides of her head, and gently moved her toward his lips. Her soft, rose petal lips met his dry ones. They wouldn't unlock.

The next few hours were everything Kayla wished for. She told Russell, "Don't let go of me. You have seven years' worth of affection to give."

"Don't worry. You're stuck to me."

CHAPTER 3

DEMONS AFOOT

Russell's returning home was a great joy and challenge for Kayla and Alexis. The first few days, Russell seemed happy, basking in the love in his life. They spent most of their time in restaurants – grabbing burgers with Russell's high school buddies, indulging in celebratory steak dinners with family. At night, when the threesome returned home, they were content to cuddle on the couch as a tight-knit family and simply talk or comment on whatever they randomly flipped on T.V.

But as the celebrations toned down and life resumed, Russell didn't know how to do the same.

What stole Kayla's breath was his unresponsive face. His eyes were fixed and distant; his brain sat somewhere else. Whenever she left for work, a temporary part-time job at the nursing home, she felt guilty. He was alone, helpless. She knew the transition was jarring for him. But the more she tried to help, the more damage she did.

One night, she saw his silhouette in the kitchen. His left hand extended by about five inches, ending in a point…Kayla perked up.

He was holding a knife.

He went to prison, but he's not a criminal, she told herself. At her nervousness, she realized how sad it was that she had to remind herself of his innocence. Russell walked toward

Kayla…only to grab a can of Campbell's soup. Wielding the knife, Russell arched his arm back and started stabbing it into the top of the can.

"Wait, wait, wait," said Kayla, scrambling off the couch and rushing over to help. "You know we have a can opener, right?" She pulled it out of the drawer and performed the act correctly. "See?"

Russell was silent.

"It's okay. It's…easy to forget these things…" Kayla didn't really think so, and it showed in her voice.

Russell's mouth was a thin line. He didn't look at her. Popping the door of the microwave open, he set the whole can in and clicked the soup button. Kayla was too worried by his blank expression, on the verge of boiling over with frustration, to notice.

Then the sparks flew.

"Russell! No!" Kayla hurriedly stopped the microwave. "Metal in the microwave, buddy." She tried to speak in a lighthearted tone. "Duh!"

Russell impassive face finally broke into an expression. "I don't need you to be my personal guard and maid, Kayla," he said with a scoff.

This hurt Kayla. "I'm trying to help out, make the transition easy…"

Russell instantly reverted back to being a robot. Saying nothing, he scooped up the can and dumped it in the trash, clearly upset – but his was incomparable to Kayla's at that moment.

Days passed. Russell was physically near to her, yet emotionally billions of miles away. He was still back in prison mentally. He took long walks around the trailer park, not even saying hi to Dorothy when she shouted out to him. He absentmindedly sat on the couch. He looked uncomfortable, like he was a germophobe sitting in a doctor's crowded waiting room.

Alexis slunk out of her room and bit her lip. She stood near Russell with her hands clasped. Kayla wondered if Alexis noticed the change or was too clueless on how her father's natural demeanor was. Slyly sitting beside him on the couch, she asked in a pleading voice, "Can we watch *American Idol?*"

Russell looked like someone just woke him up. "Oh, yeah. That sounds great."

"It *is* great! You just wait." Alexis swung her legs on the couch and excitedly turned the T.V. on. She just knew she had a television companion who wasn't picky.

But Kayla knew this wasn't the same man she married. She half-expected something of this magnitude, but she didn't know just how bad it would be. They couldn't connect like they used to at all. He always turned his back to her in bed, saying how tired he was. Kayla wondered if it were the effect of depression.

When Kayla got a call back for a job at the neonatal unit in the nearby hospital, all her fears and worries swept away. This was another hard-earned reward, and she was ecstatic. Hanging up the phone, her chest swelled with pride.

"Russell," she said, shoulders rising to just under her ears, grinning ear to ear. "Guess what?"

Not glancing up from the news, he asked what in a dull voice. Kayla skipped over, standing directly in front of him. "I got a job! I'll be a nurse in the neonatal unit at the hospital down the road!"

Searching expectantly into Russell's face, she was aghast to see his face falling.

"That's great. I'm happy for you." His voice was flat. Bitter.

At Russell's response, Kayla's heart fell. "Thanks."

Eyes burning with tears, she backed away then turned to face the door. She wiped her face with her shirtsleeve and mumbled, "I'm going to tell Dorothy."

She ran outside, sight blurred with plentiful tears, and climbed the steps to her front door. Hurling herself into Dorothy's living room, she found her sitting on her tweed recliner with a ballpoint pen and grocery list. Kayla let the tears flow, the salty droplets pooling around her lips.

Dorothy stood up and put her hands on her hips. "What he do? That miserable little…"

Kayla shook her head, not wanting to hear it. All she could do was bury her face on Dorothy's shoulder, her curled hair sticking to her tear-stained cheeks.

After a long talk with Dorothy, Kayla knew this boiled down to insecurity. With his record, it would be much more difficult to secure a job, especially because the unemployment rate was so high.

"I understand, but he has to lay it all on the table! Communication and honesty are the ingredients for success in the relationship. How can we shake off our baggage without it?" she had said.

During dinner, Alexis happily chatted about school; Russell was quiet. Kayla glanced at him when their daughter asked for input, hoping he'd be more engaging. He wasn't. He was solely focused on the act of chewing. Her stomach churned at the sight of him, so uninterested in his daughter's life.

One night, the explosion brewing in Kayla threatened to spill out. She laid in bed with Russell, whose back was turned to her. She saw the pattern of light from the window fall on his defensive shoulders. Her desire for him to emotionally engage her, and be loved physically, drove her to speak her mind.

"So," she began straightforwardly, "I'm gathering that you'd rather be in the cell than with your family."

Russell slowly turned to her, his face darkened, and said, "Um, no. I never want to go back to that *hell*."

"Well you're still in it. You can't give over to joy anymore. I'm here for you — always have been, always will be — but you have to try." Before she knew it, the tears that were dammed up now overflowed, flooding her face. "It's like, who is this man? Is this really my husband? Alexis's father? I thought you'd be a little happier to see us, because we've been waiting for this moment, running it over and over in our minds, for *years*."

Russell appeared taken aback.

"It's great that you actually seem to feel something!" she blurted out. The sobs that built up in her throat the past few days finally spilled out. Russell's face, hardened with lines, softened at his wife's emotional breakdown.

"That's not it, okay?" he mumbled. Turning toward her, he opened his mouth, then closed it again, hesitant to speak, his emotions behind bars.

"I can't deal with this. I've been waiting to love you for years. This isn't worth it."

Russell's firm countenance crumbled. He took Kayla in his arms and held her as they both tried regaining control of their emotions.

"I'm scared," was all Russell said. He hugged her tighter. Kayla mouthed *I know*. Minutes passed, maybe even an hour, where Kayla just listened to his heartbeat and dabbed her eyes with his shirt.

Finally, Russell dropped the bomb on her. "Why did you even wait for me?" The ugly question shattered the jagged silence in the room. Others had asked this question countless times, but Kayla couldn't believe Russell would ask. Her mouth was slightly agape.

Russell continued. "Did you have an affair with anyone while I wasn't around? I mean, who could blame you? I guess it would be too much to ask to refuse. I wasn't worth it."

This pierced Kayla. Her words to Dorothy about honesty flashed across her mind. She also remembered the story of "Othello" and didn't want her husband to turn into that character, driven mad by jealousy. She took a deep breath and managed to say, "If I told you that nobody ever liked me or that I didn't like one of them while you were away, I'd be lying. But I did *not* have an affair with anyone. *You* are the only person I love and want to spend the rest of my life with. I knew that quickly after meeting you, and that hasn't changed. Don't you understand? If my faithfulness doesn't show it, I don't know what will. All I want now is for us to be a family again."

Russell sat in melancholic silence for a few minutes. Kayla hoped her mention of Dr. Leon wouldn't upset him too greatly. After the suspense-permeated silence, Russell said, "I know. It's just hard to believe you would do that for me."

"Of course I would," said Kayla. "I married you. I love you. And, truth be told, I feel somewhat responsible for you going to prison. I guess we both did desperate things to be with one another."

Russell's hands crept on Kayla's face, and he entwined his fingers through her hair. Pulling her close, he kissed her. Nothing too passionate, but gentle, as if he were venturing into new territory. With their first steps with physical intimacy, they came to terms with his insecurity and the difficulty of plugging back into life. But they would work together.

From then on, Russell made a concerted effort. He still looked like he was struggling against quicksand, struggling to keep from sinking into self-pity and hopelessness. Kayla was more receptive to these moods. Placing a hand on his shoulder, she said, "I'm always available to talk. I love you."

When Russell's aura darkened, and he was clearly lost in his worries, sometimes Kayla couldn't rouse him out. She left him alone. There were times only Russell could work out what he needed to. Kayla only hoped it would improve around Christmas, which was fast approaching.

He was exacerbated at night. After Alexis went to sleep, Kayla found Russell sobbing on the couch. This was the first outpouring of emotion since their reconciliatory discussion, but it was far worse. Knees drawn up in fetal position, Russell leaned his head on the wall, right under the crack. His long fingers were tangled in his hair, tensed, scratching his scalp.

"Russ!" Kayla swooped down to him and gently placed her hands on his knees. She rubbed them consolingly. He shrunk away from her.

"I'm nothing," he said. Kayla was alarmed. She had never heard him speak like this.

"That's absolutely not true. You've had difficult times – we both have – and we'll get through them."

Russell shook his head and said, "I just don't think I'm going to be able to be enough for you."

Kayla's hand felt cold, clammy, and her stomach churned. "Stop speaking like that." As she saw the shaking, vulnerable figure, Kayla hoped he was just all talk. She thought the sight of this broken figure would in turn break *her* – but it increased her resolve to be strong.

"All I've done is add stress to your life."

Kayla rubbed his leg harder and lifted his chin. She already knew her answer, recited it in her mind, many a time, if need be. "No. You've made me happier than anyone else. I know what true happiness is, because I've known profound sadness. I know the value of patience. I'm a wiser individual. I've been on all ends of the spectrum of human emotion. So I recognize that all bad times pass, and something valuable will arise from them."

Russell's empty look of hopelessness implied he wasn't so sure.

Kayla exhaled and searched within her for answers. "Russ, I've been thinking about myself the last few months – how you should make me feel, how you should be excited for me, how I don't feel loved. I've been selfish. Just let me know what I can do for you, and I'll stop thinking of what you can do for me." She broke off. The emotion trembled in her voice. "If you want to leave, so be it. But I'll wish for you here, every day, and won't stop loving you. It's impossible to stop now."

With that, Kayla stopped trying to change him. She gave him the space needed to regroup. Coping with Russell's demons was enough for him at that point. He didn't need to know she was also waging war against them

CHAPTER 4

CAN IT BE RESOLVED?

When their emotional connections became nonexistent, physical connections increased. It was the Band-Aid hastily slapped onto their relationship. Kayla made sure Alexis would never know.

"I'm going to Mom's," said Russell one day, grabbing his sweatshirt and holding onto the doorknob. Kayla glanced up from the dishes she was doing in the kitchen and pursed her lips. "Alright, then."

"I wanna come see Grandma, too," said Alexis. They were especially close – it worried Kayla that Alexis knew Veronica and Mrs. Mancini more than Russell and her own mom. She had hung on them during Christmas, and it didn't help they bought her better gifts. Kayla would work hard to change the dynamic as soon as Russell escaped from between the rock and a hard place. They would reacquaint each other with being a tight-knit family.

Russell looked slightly annoyed, as if he wanted to see Mrs. Mancini on his own and on the fly, but he thought better of it. "Alright, Alexis. Hurry up."

Pushing her brown bangs aside, Alexis slipped on her worn sneakers and ran up beside her father. Russell smiled; nothing seemed to change his opinion of spending time with Alexis. That, or he was beginning to try hard to conceal his complex emotions.

Yes, thought Kayla. *Time to run around in my underwear.*

She grinned facetiously. Being alone was a new occurrence for her. She considered it her new second love. She figured she could recharge her batteries before her Skype date with Breeana at 3 p.m. (for Breeana, it would be just before she went out for a night in the city).

Soon Kayla saw Breeana's beaming face lit up on the computer screen.

"Hey lover girl!" said Breeana, flashing her white teeth and waving, charm bracelets tinkling with her movement. "How ya doing?"

"Feeling pretty tired, working like a dog, the usual post-college life. And you? How do I say that in French?"

"*Et vous?*"

"Ay vooz....I sound too American. French is not my language."

"French doesn't come naturally to everyone." Breeana laughed.

"You're right. There are too many letters that they don't even pronounce."

They shared another round of laughter before Breeana continued. "I'm doing okay. Still seeing Stefan. We spent New Year's together, and we're going out tonight!"

Her curls bounced excitedly; her makeup was so thick that Kayla said, "Make sure he doesn't choke on all the Chloe perfume you're wearing. I can almost see the cloud around you."

"How'd you know what I'm wearing?"

"It just made sense with the rest of your ensemble."

When the levity filtered out of the conversation, Kayla explained her problems with Russell. "Time for the depressing stuff," she began.

Breeana listened attentively as Kayla relayed everything, but her face was hard to read.

"He just spends more and more time with his mom. Like he needs to get away from me. Thankfully he takes Alexis along, but I don't know. It makes me sick just thinking about it – it literally makes me sick. I can't eat."

Breeana toyed with her costume ring and nodded almost imperceptibly. "How long has he been home? Six months?"

"Yeah."

"Well I'd give it time. He's still adjusting. I can't imagine what he's gone through."

"I know that logically, but it feels different. He keeps saying he doesn't know if he can stay with me. It kills me."

"Are you physical?"

Kayla blushed. "Oh yeah."

"Get it, Kayla. I don't see the problem."

Kayla groaned. "It's more like a coping mechanism for him. There's no emotion."

"Well that's more complicated than I thought. New topic. Are you guys going to ever move out now that you have a job?"

Kayla sighed. "Whenever things are more stable, I guess. I don't want to give Russell too much change at once. *I'm* ready, though."

As they continued to talk, Breeana floated back to her topic of choice: Stefan, her flame from Bordeaux. Life was so simple for her: teaching English in France, completing her masters degree soon, and spending ample time in Paris with a sophisticated Frenchman. When they got off, Kayla couldn't help but feel jealous.

That night, she shoveled her green beans, stacking and crossing them in hopes of making a little log cabin on her plate. Most of the food was uneaten. The tenuous green-bean cabin fell over as Kayla abruptly knocked her fork into it as her husband and daughter entered the trailer.

Alexis ran in and asked to use Kayla's cell phone to call a friend. She nodded and watched as Alexis retreated into her room. When the door closed, Russell looked at her with his hands in his pockets.

"I'm moving back in with Mom," he muttered as he shifted his eyes away.

Kayla's fork fell with a clatter. "What?"

"I...don't want to do this anymore."

The knots in Kayla's stomach tightened and churned. "What are you saying?"

"I don't want to do this to you anymore." His eyes filled with tears. "I don't want to drag you down. I've done it long enough. Don't you understand – you have a college degree and a respectful profession. I am a jobless bum with a criminal record. I am just not right for you. Kayla, we don't have to pretend we are a happy, perfect couple..."

In a daze, Kayla stood up and gripped the table for support as Russell's words started snowballing.

"I see you. You're unhappy. You're worried about me. We're trying to make this work and we just…can't."

"I can't believe you feel that way," she said. She gripped the table harder, unable to process his words. "*I* don't feel that way."

"You do. I see it. And who are we to say we work? It's been years. Are we holding onto a…a delusion? I don't know, but I also know that I love you all the same, even though life changed and…I just know that I'm too much trouble. I'm lost."

Kayla stared at him. Her stomach churned harder and harder. Bile rose to her throat. Trying to swallow it, she realized it was more forceful than she realized.

Next thing she knew, she stood over the sink, holding her hair back, tears stinging her eyes not only from the vomit but from her flurried emotions. Squinting her eyes shut, she immediately sunk to the floor. Russell was leaving. Russell didn't want to do it anymore. Even after all her waiting.

She rested her feverish head on her knees on the kitchen floor. Russell pled to talk, caressing her shoulders. She pulled away. It was coming. She saw it but struggled against it.

It was really ending

Dorothy walked over in her high heels, which she had to really tug out of the moist ground from the morning's rain as they pierced through the dirt. She scraped the heels on the metallic steps leading up to the trailer. With a quick rap on the door, she slowly twisted it open.

"Hello?" she shouted. Alexis was at school and Kayla had her day off from the neonatal unit. Strangely, she wasn't on the couch or at the dinner table. Puzzled, Dorothy clopped over to the closed bedroom door and knocked once again.

"Yo, Kay?"

Silence. Dorothy frowned. There was no way Kayla would leave her door unlocked. She knocked again.

"Aaa," said Kayla. She sounded like she was gargling. That's when Dorothy opened the door and saw her friend laying in a ball on the side of the bed, thick black rings under her eyes and her messy brown hair spread on the pillow – more like a pile of dead branches than Kayla's former tresses.

"Girl what's wrong with you?"

Kayla stared, unsmiling. "So I look that bad, huh?"

As Dorothy cracked up – that was an *understatement* – Kayla rolled her eyes and her lip corners tilted up with the shadow of a smile. Then she just pointed to the bedside table. Dorothy peeked over; there was a small white stick there.

"What about that table?" she asked.

"Look closer."

Dorothy did. There, on the stick, was a happy face. She slowly turned to Kayla with her mouth wide open. "Ohh lord…" Her eyes began welling with tears. "You're gonna be a mommy again!"

Kayla's eyes welled with the other variety of tears. Stopping what she was doing, Dorothy stooped down and wrapped her arms around Kayla. She tried to hide the anger that boiled within her at Russell – after watching Kayla suffer so long without him, the fact he wanted a separation "for her sake" (which Dorothy thought was complete crap if she ever heard it) was despicable.

"Ya gotta tell him," Dorothy said. "Even knowing what I do about him, you just gotta."

As Kayla dabbed her eyes on the pillowcase, she felt déjà vu – it was creepily reminiscent of Veronica telling her to tell Russell back when they had Alexis. Prior to all the mess that occurred three years later.

Somehow, for some reason, Kayla had a sick feeling in her stomach, and it sure wasn't morning sickness.

CHAPTER 5

IS IT THE BEGINNING
OR THE END?

It was week three without Russell, and Kayla was pregnant. Waking up to make her 7 a.m. shift at the hospital became increasingly difficult as she suffered the morning sickness of the first trimester.

As her alarm went off that morning, she hunched over and buried her head in her hands. She wiggled each toe on the carpet, surrounded by crumbs from nibbling crackers in bed. Her stomach was unsteady, as if she stepped out of a rollercoaster, "And all I did was sit up," moaned Kayla. "I need to 'man up'...ironically."

As she huddled over her mug of decaf tea at the table, Alexis pranced in.

"Mom, you look like a zombie."

"I feel like one, too. Now don't get too critical, or I'll eat your face."

Alexis grabbed a pop tart out of the pantry and smirked "Are we going now? You usually rush me out."

Kayla sighed and rose up. "Yes, come on, dear."

As they stepped outside, Kayla felt like the sun shone exponentially brighter, burning her eyes and quickly heating her body. It was an unusually warm day for San Francisco in Feburary.

"Forget zombie, I feel like a vampire," Kayla said. As they walked to the bus stop, Kayla cursed herself for forgetting her water bottle as the heat bore down on her. She kissed Alexis good-bye as she went toward the school bus, and Kayla continued onward to her own bus. Her heart beat weakly in her sickly body, and the tea threatened to reappear.

It's gonna take a miracle to get through my shift, she thought.

Feeling increasingly weak and nauseated, she was unaware of her surroundings. She felt like she was trudging underwater, fighting against a current and struggling to pull her legs from the muck underfoot. She wished she could eat. Food lost its palatability when Russell left.

Russell. She knew she shouldn't think about him. The weight of her mind threatened to crush her as she retreated further into it. The physical world didn't matter. The Doppler effect was failing her – the voices around her sounded faint and deep. Even when they were close by.

Was that light green?

Sounds…so distant. Even the honking of a horn as she crossed the street…

The next thing Kayla knew, she was face to face with a black truck.

Then darkness.

The ambulance took Kayla to a nearby hospital where they tried to stabilize her condition. She had broken legs and ribs and was unconscious. Her face was skinned up, she had a large, scabbed lump near her eye, and untold damage elsewhere. Kayla's vital signs were extremely weak and unstable.

The ER staff doctor in that small hospital, Dr. Patel, called and discussed the case with his colleague, Dr. Johenssen at the other hospital, which was one of the best hospitals in the Bay area with the reputation for superior emergency and ICU care.

"I recommend we transfer her as soon as you stabilize her a bit," said Dr. Johenssen.

"Right – I knew that from the start," agreed Dr. Patel.

With that, they transferred Kayla over there. Kayla's condition was so severe that whether she could make it was questionable. Even if she did, she might be in a vegetative state. As Dr. Johenssen was the chief staff doctor in the ER and ICU departments in that hospital, he immediately examined her. Time was of the essence. After he evaluated Kayla's condition, he ordered many tests. He cautiously made his diagnosis and shared the prognosis with her family, who filtered into the hospital at once. Since Kayla's unconscious, Dr. Johenssen decided to get Dr. Shapiro in Neurology involved.

CHAPTER 6

RUSSELL
WHAT IS THIS WORLD?

For those who are released from imprisonment, they never truly elude captivity. The mind is the true form of solitary confinement. Casting off its shackles is sometimes a lifelong endeavor.

"Do you want anything?" asked his mom, poking her curly head out of the kitchen doorway. Kayla described Mrs. Mancini's hair as '80s. "She never escaped that decade," she once told Russell with a snicker.

"After the third time, I guess I'll consent," replied Russell.

"Good!" said the portly Mrs. Mancini. "Because I made you some rice balls."

Russell groaned. True to Italian tradition, eating was the Mancini family's "cure-all." If he was sad, mad, or happy, the answer was always, "It sounds like it's time for food."

Russell slumped back in his mom's squeaky, white leather sofa. The TV tray was over by his father's chair...he'd let his mother bring it over. He crossed his arms over his gray sweatshirt and absentmindedly stared at his mother's porcelain collection in the glass cabinet.

Once his mother brought him food, Russell sliced open the fried, cheesy ball of rice and meat. Aromatic steam reached for his nostrils. He missed these. Too bad his mother was trying to stuff him like a pig. She hoped it would cajole him to talk about why he was never home with Kayla. But she was afraid – afraid to talk to her own son now. Everyone worried it would cause him more stress. God only knew what would happen after that—maybe he'd crack. At first irritating and isolating, he soon became insecure with the notion.

Was he so certain he wasn't already cracking?

The phone rang, so Mrs. Mancini got up and left Russell with her soap operas on the TV. Kayla popped into Russell's head again… *What a melodramatic load of crap! All these doctors are too busy romancing the nurses to pay attention to their patients. Let's hope this is just an old-lady fantasy and not real life.*

"Veronica? Yes… Russell is here. Hold on – Russell, it's Veronica."

Looking at his mother with a furrowed brow, he wondered why on earth she'd be calling. To scold him? To tell him what a good-for-nothing he was? Regardless, he accepted the phone.

"Hello?"

"Russell." Veronica's tone was soft, urgent, like she was making a clandestine phone call. "It's Kayla."

"What about her?"

"She's…" Veronica stopped and released a shuddering sigh. Russell suddenly felt more numb than usual. "She's in the hospital."

Silence again.

"She's been…*hit* by a car."

"I-is s-she okay?" His body started convulsing.

"She's not responsive."

Russell didn't need to know anything else. He dropped his forehead against the kitchen doorframe. He whacked it again for good measure, making sure he wasn't dreaming.

Veronica told him the room number at the hospital. Russell hung up without another word. Slumping to the ground, his mother walked over to him, her face etched with concern.

"Get Alexis," was all he said.

Nothing was real as Russell jumped on the bus. His mind ignored all else except the singular goal of making it to Kayla. There was absolutely nothing else in the world.

As he punched the elevator buttons, inhaled the antiseptic air of the hospital, and saw flowers for sale on the bottom floor, his brain started absorbing the shock. His breathing became more and more rapid as he ascended each floor. And then the ICU…

Running down the halls, he knew immediately which room was Kayla's. There was Joycelyn, Veronica, and Dorothy. And then his breathing stopped at the sight of her.

There she was—her body, marred almost beyond recognition. Her face was swollen and red, while her left eye was a bruised purple. The temple on her right side was scabbed, and her arm was in a sling. What stole his breath for another good minute were her closed eyes and the slow rise and fall of her chest—so tenuous, as if she struggled to get them out. Part of her face was covered by the oxygen mask.

Kayla was in critical condition and the prognosis from the doctors was very poor. Whether she would make it was questionable; she might be in a vegetative state even if she made it. She was on life support. The thought of not being able to see her or talk to her again terrified Russell beyond words, along with the rest of the family. Russell recalled the last time they were together and the last words he said to her…the regret and pain was killing him. How he wished he had done it differently.

The doctor turned toward him with an impassive, almost cold look. He wore black rimmed glasses, had longer, brown hair, and looked to be in his late twenties or early thirties. He softly told Russell upon arrival, "She's in a coma."

The sight of Russell must have been so pitiable that Veronica ran up and hugged him. Too shocked to notice the shock of that act, he kept his eyes on Kayla. That's when the guilt settled in. That's when the relentless questions attacked and stuck to his mind like wasps on flypaper.

Rubbing his face, he wondered how he would ever tell Alexis.

"Just keep her at your place. I don't want her to see," Russell told Mrs. Mancini.

"That's her mother! She needs to be near her…maybe *Kayla* needs that!"

His mother was predictably emotional. He just wanted to make sure that if Alexis saw her, she would be stable...but if it wasn't maybe that was all the more reason to let her see.

Russell saw some gut-wrenching sights in prison: a man stealing off another man's tray at dinner. The ensuing fight, where they almost killed each other. The rashes that nagged him as he curled into a ball in bed, for which he got no treatment. Having to be constantly alert—especially in the shower. Witnessing rape. Wishing he could disappear. Being afraid to close his eyes because he didn't know if he could trust the men in his cell. Never fully sleeping, rarely having an appetite or eating. Sick paranoia that refused to leave, the mental whispers that Kayla was gone forever. Never seeing his daughter grow. Weighed down by resulting misery. Fears of the present slowly giving way to fears of the future.

These things he never told Kayla. How could she know the lasting impact? One didn't know just how terrifying it was, how it changes a person, until they're there.

But he held that against her.

He couldn't handle himself. How could he expect Kayla to?

But as she lay, bloodied and comatose, he felt like a fool. Isn't that what landed him in prison anyway? He was a hopeless fool.

Shuffling into the room, he sat by Kayla. Veronica sat by her side, stroking Kayla's hair and mumbling everything that came to her mind. "Just think about Alexis, if you can. Alexis loves you. We love you. We can't wait to see you again. Just make the effort…wake up." Veronica whispered by Kayla's bedside, rambling the whole time Russell was there.

Her hand was directly in front of him, and he couldn't help but grab it and squeeze so hard that maybe, maybe she could wake up. Her arms were attached to tubes.

Robert, Veronica's husband, placed his large, comforting hands on her shoulders. Veronica looked haggard, with deep, black lines under her eyes. It would take a lot of soothing and encouragement for her to leave Kayla's side.

"What if she can hear me? I don't want to stop talking to her," cried Veronica. Sobbing, she flung herself in Robert's arms as he patted her back and held her close. Robert's tan face was impassive. There were no words to soothe the hurt of Kayla's beloved sister; the uncertainty agonized everyone.

Dorothy remained by herself to the side, her face unmoving and devoid of the colors that she was known for.

"Please, baby. I'll be here watching her and talking to her the whole time you go back." Veronica nodded once, trying to wrap her mind around the idea of leaving. Then, Robert tried to lighten the mood just a little. "We don't want Kayla to smell you, after all. Go get yourself some food. Kayla would be force-feeding you right now."

Veronica couldn't smile, but her eyes looked slightly less empty at Robert's reminder. She finally left unwillingly.

Now it was just Russell and Dorothy, but for all he knew, Kayla was the only one who existed at that moment. His stomach felt tangled with withheld emotions and a cold burning—as if such a sensation were possible. Squeezing Kayla's hand, feeling its warmth, he tried to derive comfort.

"You know something," said Dorothy after a half-hour of standing as they both stared at Kayla. Robert had gone to the bathroom and momentarily left them alone. "She was pregnant with your child."

Russell had been certain he couldn't feel any more devastation; it was already too much to handle. Upon Dorothy's news, he was regretful to have been so woefully wrong.

CHAPTER 7

BONDS ARE BORN

Days and nights were one and the same to Russell, whose world was timeless. He went home when his mother begged him to come, see his daughter, and shower. Soon enough, Alexis came to the hospital with Mrs. Mancini. She deserved that.

Russell turned his heavy head up to her as she walked in. What a sight for an eleven-year-old—she didn't seem to know *how* to take it. Russell felt awake at that moment. She was approaching her teenage years; he could see so much of Kayla in her at that particular moment. Parts of her were the exact same: strong shoulders, wispy brown hair, and that tiny nose. It almost broke him. He took her in his arms and whispered, "She will wake up. It's a matter of waiting."

That's what everyone was telling Alexis. "She's in a coma, but she will wake up." Alexis took it as a good sign she hadn't passed after all that time. She was quiet, but she didn't appear devastated. She actually could not comprehend the meaning of "coma." She took it as a "deep sleep." She was going to Google it later on.

"To be young," murmured Dorothy, slinging her imitation Louis Vuitton purse over her shoulder.

If only Alexis knew about her unborn sibling…

Russell mourned the child as if he/she had already been born. His life felt like it was drawing to a close, even in his young age. It was the unspoken elephant in the room—Veronica's sobs were stronger lately, and Mrs. Mancini shed more than her fair share of tears upon hearing the news that Russell hated to share.

Russell's eyes darted back and forth as the terrifying possibility arose that they could be waiting for Kayla to wake up for a long, long time. Then came the startling realization that he was what Alexis had left with Kayla gone. He would take her place as the single parent. The single parent to a child he hardly knew. No, he couldn't stand himself, couldn't stand what his life was amounting to—but it wasn't all about his life.

That's when Russell tucked away his insecurity, at least for the time being. Alexis gave him purpose. She was his distraction. She was what he had in life should things turn… ill.

As Alexis sat by Kayla's bedside, she looked curious. Kayla's IV was still in, but the purple blotch on her eye was noticeably smaller and faded. Alexis hadn't seen the worst of it. Thank God.

Russell sighed, wiped his hands on the thigh of his jeans, and stood up. "Hey," he said to Alexis. "What do you say we get out of here? I don't know about you, but I've had enough hospital food."

Not as bad as the bony chicken from prison. He shook the thought away.

Alexis bit her lip. "Well, where do you wanna go?"

"I like everything. You choose." Russell stuck his hands in his pockets like the lanky teen he once was.

"I wanna milkshake. The Burger Boat?"

Russell felt Veronica wince across from them at the mention of her old employer, and he almost smiled for the first time in weeks.

"Let's go, then."

Their lunch turned into a half-day away. Russell ordered Alexis a large milkshake, which caused her jaw to drop to the table. "Mom never lets me do that," she said.

"Eh, my treat."

Russell ended up drinking half of it, but Alexis's girlish delight thawed his heart. He pushed away the mental image of a younger brother or sister sitting by her, staring up with large, curious eyes.

An order of curly fries and chicken strips later, they decided to walk around the outlet mall to stretch their legs. Shopping wasn't Russell's favorite, but walking felt good, and sightseeing was a distraction. They didn't speak much, but Russell found himself wanting to ruffle her hair, but somehow felt it was too familiar a gesture for someone a bit unfamiliar. As they approached the hospital, Alexis smiled gratefully. That was enough for Russell.

When they walked back into Kayla's room, Russell realized the brooding doctor with the black-rimmed glasses was gone.

"What happened to our guy?" he asked Veronica.

Her lips pursed, like she didn't want to say. "Well…he couldn't emotionally detach from her," she said slowly. "He wanted to work on her but…"

"It was too much," finished Joycelyn, looking up at Russell impassively. Her hair was wrapped up in a bun, and she wore her dance jacket.

It took awhile for Russell to understand, but then all became clear. An hour or so later, Robert carelessly mentioned that the nurses heard Dr. Leon calling Kayla's name over and over again, begging Kayla to wake up while he was attending her. Russell remembered that Kayla did her externship at that hospital. She worked in the Emergency Room. That's where she had been that first day she was brought in, when he saw the doctor the first time. The doctor carried over as she settled in the hospital, strangely, which was rare. At the time Russell didn't think much of it.

But he must have known her, he realized.

That might have been…Him. The other guy Kayla liked.

Maybe that's a stretch, Russell thought. But he didn't believe himself. It appeared to be common knowledge that the doctor and Kayla were previously acquainted—even Joycelyn was aware of that!

He couldn't handle any more unfavorable notions. He stopped thinking right there. By that point, Russell promised himself he would become an expert in blocking his thoughts with an impenetrable, mental brick wall.

Since Dr. Leon was one of the residency doctors under Dr. Johenssen's supervision in ER/ICU department, he was assigned to Kayla's case. He was emotionally disturbed while trying to be completely professional when he saw Kayla. Doctors were accustomed to dividing their emotions and their logic under stressful situations, and Dr. Leon mastered it—or so he thought. He had thought of Kayla frequently since that fateful night, but he would never have expected to see her under such circumstances.

Tragedies don't play favorites, he thought bitterly. *It can affect anyone at the most unexpected moment.*

Kayla had been in coma for more than two weeks. Each day, Dr. Leon's hands balled into tense fists at the sight of her. How could fate have been so cruel? The results were painfully ambiguous. Who knew if Kayla could hear him or anyone? Kayla's sister was constantly hovering over her and letting her tears freely fall. If Kayla could hear, well, he wanted to make sure she could enjoy herself.

One day, Dr. Leon walked into Dr. Johenssens's office and shared his ideas to Dr. Johenssen.

"Whatever you do," Dr. Johenssen advised, "Just contact Dr. Shapiro first and double check." So he did. Dr. Shapiro's response was simple.

"Go ahead and try it. Nothing to lose." If anything, it had the potential of calming the family.

Dr. Leon proceeded with his plan. First he received consent from Kayla's family. Veronica nodded quickly, and Russell's empty eyes were emotionless as he said, "Okay," and signed the consent form.

First Dr. Leon downloaded classical music from iTunes, mostly from the classical and romantic eras, with composers like Mozart, Medelssohn, Beethoven and Chopin, to his iPod because he had read some articles that classical music was good for babies' brain development. If it was good for baby's brains, he assumed that it should be good for Kayla's brain in that condition. Then he chose some fun articles from the Yahoo news page to read aloud to her.

Every night, after his shift was over, he brought his iPod and reading material to Kayla's room.

"What are you doing here off duty?" a nurse asked with an ironic smile. He explained to other nurses and his staff doctor that Kayla used to do her internship at ER department while she was a nursing student.

"She was always very kind and helpful to me," he said softly.

He would adjust the volume of the iPod and put the earphones up to Kayla's ear. After twenty-to-thirty minutes of music, he turned off the iPod and read articles to keep Kayla up to date with the world. He made sure they were always more jocular in nature, never anything too depressing. Lord knew she had enough of that.

By the end of the night, he couldn't help himself anymore. The hour of a silent Kayla got to him. He would call Kayla's name gently and beg her to wake up. He did this night after night. To avoid any suspicion and misunderstandings, he always left the room door wide open so other nurses could see him easily.

His fondness for Kayla never remained a secret.

Upon learning the news, Russell rarely left Kayla's side. She continued to heal each day, but she was still in the dark. Could she hear anything? Was she dreaming? Could she feel his touch, even if she couldn't make sense of it?

At long last, Kayla's mother came to visit her daughter. Kayla briefly mentioned how she and her mother became distant after her mother moved to Oklahoma to live with her husband (mostly for the money, though Kayla wouldn't speak about it too much), but apparently the rift between Veronica and Kayla's mother was even stronger. She waited to tell her after two weeks' time.

When Kayla's mother came in, she had a huge purse that more closely resembled a duffel bag, bursting with who knows what. She wore a velour Juicy Couture jumpsuit—her idea of casual. Her brown hair had gold highlights and looked permed.

At that moment, Veronica and her mother seemed to put aside their differences as they hugged and looked at Kayla. Her mother's mouth dropped and she turned her face toward Veronica as they embraced once again. Veronica's eyes welled up with tears as she whispered the unspeakable—what must have been about the baby. That's when Kayla's mother could no longer hold herself up. Russell rushed over and helped set her down in a chair.

"Oh my god," shrieked Kayla's mother, burying her face in her manicured hands. Russell could immediately tell that maybe this woman didn't make the best choices for herself and in interest of her family, but she had feelings and certainly loved her children.

The hours added up to ten. It was late, and Robert was speaking with Veronica on the phone.

"No, I won't go. I know we've gone through this, but it's been such a long time...she'll have to wake up, something will have to happen!"

Veronica started crying again. Russell went with his instincts and stood up, putting his arm around Veronica. She quickly leaned against him, in desperate need of support.

"I...I don't know," she said shakily. "I just don't want to leave her."

Russell interrupted her conversation. "I'm here. Go home and be with your kids."

"Hold on, Rob." She held the phone away from her tear-streaked face. Her hair was messy, and Russell could see the first lines of aging on her face, seemingly increased over the time period. "What?"

"Hang up the phone."

Veronica said, "Call you back," before somehow doing what Russell told her.

"Veronica, I promise you I'm not leaving her side. Not for a moment. I will tell you at the very first sign something happens. Absolutely *any* change. You have my word." His eyes blazed. Veronica somehow found comfort in his stony demeanor. Among them, he somehow stayed the strongest.

"You have children," he said, "and they need you. Alexis doesn't have her mother with her. She *really* needs you. Can you do that for me? Can you be with Alexis, be there for her as a mother?"

Veronica's eyes glistened and she turned to her mother, as if recognizing the parallels. As if on cue, Kayla's mother stood up. "I can go back and be with the kids…"

Veronica shook her head quickly. "No. You haven't gotten much time with Kayla. I'll go back."

Russell gave her a hug. "Thank you." He was overwhelmed with gratitude. Alexis needed someone that knew her better than he did. She needed the nurture and care of a mother.

As Veronica left, Kayla's mother looked at him with tired yet rapt eyes. He glanced up at her before returning to Kayla. Her eyelids and skin around the area of her closed eyes were now yellow, free of the stormy, dark purple that had discolored them. Definite healing. Her arm was still in a cast. Her legs… well, time would tell.

"You know," Kayla's mother began with a raspy whisper. "I like you."

Her message of approval was stark in the uneasy silence of the room. They looked at each other for a moment before Kayla's mom added, "and so does Veronica."

"Wow," was all Russell could say. "Thank you."

Approval from Kayla's protective older sister was a shock indeed. They liked him…but if only he could like himself.

CHAPTER 8

THE DAWN ARRIVES

It had been four weeks since the accident. There was no sign of Kayla returning to them, but her condition was stabilized.

Why did I do what I did?

The regret circulated in Russell's head relentlessly. It was part of his everyday routine, along with spending time in Kayla's hospital room in shifts with Veronica. The heart monitor was slow, but constant. The maddening beeps were a comfort and an annoyance at the same time—Kayla was alive but not *living*.

It was a sunny yet chilly morning in early April. Kayla had now been in a coma for five weeks. The nurse came in to check Kayla's condition and put all her vital information on the tablet. Since the change of health care regulation, all the medical information had to be electronically recorded. It was much easier for the nurse to concentrate on her tasks, as Kayla's family had not arrived yet. There was only the beeping and electronic sounds characteristic of a hospital floating around her.

Suddenly, she heard a weak voice.

"Where am I?"

The nurse pivoted around and looked back. Kayla's eyes were closed again, if they had ever been open. She wondered if she just thought she heard Kayla—wishful thinking, perhaps.

"What's going on here?"

There it was! Then, "Where is my daughter?"

The nurse was startled and tried to calm Kayla down.

"Shh, she will be here soon," she soothed. In the meantime, she pushed the red button to signal other nurse to come in immediately. Dr. Johenssen was promptly informed and arrived shortly. Dr. Shapiro was in a meeting.

Kayla kept asking, "Where is my daughter?" She became louder and louder the longer time passed. No one could blame her; it would be a bewildering event to wake up having been in a coma for five weeks without any memory.

Not long afterward, Veronica burst into the room with her mother closely behind her.

"Oh my gosh, I can't believe it!" Veronica shouted, spewing happy tears for the first time in her life.

"Be calm," commanded the nurse. "We don't want to overstimulate her at this time."

After Veronica's outburst, she sat with twinkling eyes, squeezing Kayla's hand until Russell joined in. When Russell saw her with her eyes open, he thought he'd cry with joy for the first time as well. Even getting out of prison wasn't nearly as exciting.

Kayla stared at him groggily, and it wasn't clear if she was glad or unwilling to see him. One thing was certain: she wanted to see Alexis with every fiber of her being.

"She's at school. I'll go get her right now," Russell said, reluctant to leave Kayla but more than obliging to satisfy any and every wish she had. Russell's parents had let him use the old family car to go back and forth since Kayla's accident. At that point, he was grateful he could jump in the car to get Alexis without having to wait for the bus.

His heart pounded, and his world was in a blur as he picked up Alexis. Neither of them talked much on the drive over. Alexis was leaning forward and hyper-alert on their way over, as if ready to jump from the car and sprint for her mother immediately.

That's just what she did. Alexis rushed into Kayla's room and was on her in an instant for a hug. Kayla wrapped her arms as tightly around Alexis as she could muster, as the tubes dangled from them.

"Don't ever go back to sleep," Alexis begged as she hugged her mother.

"Never," said Kayla.

Russell, Veronica, and Kayla's mom hovered around the bed during the scene, sharing Kleenex and tears. Though they tried to stay calm per the nurse's request, they eventually gave up. They laughed and spoke normally, if a little high pitched.

Dr. Leon was in the ER clinic attending to patients when he heard the news that Kayla had awakened.

"Wow, really?" he said at the news. Glancing up from the patient, he found it difficult to pay attention and resume work.

Hardly able to conceal his excitement, he decided to stop by her room to check it out during his lunch break. He found himself punching the elevator buttons impatiently, walking at an above-average pace to get to her room. But he quickly and quietly retreated when he saw the room filled with Kayla's family. They were all huddled together and sharing an intimate moment. He knew he would be intruding.

⚊⟵⟶⚊

Over the next few days, Kayla went through a battery of neurological and cognitive tests. The assessment from the Dr. Shapiro after studying all the test results was that Kayla had no obvious neurological damage or memory loss.

Hearing that Kayla was free of mental defects and consistently awake, her mother returned to her wealthy husband and left San Francisco. Veronica still spent plenty of time at the hospital but didn't feel the need to stick to her at all hours of the day. When Alexis went back to school, that gave Russell the much-needed alone time that he had hoped for.

Kayla sat up, propped by a few pillows and absentmindedly watching television. Russell sat in a chair by the opposite wall and took in the sight of her. Her brown hair, usually up in a ponytail, flowed on either side of her chest. Her face was fairly healed but had an unhealthy pallor. Her eyes compensated for her weak look – they looked alert, as if trying to soak in every sight she lacked during the past month.

Russell felt shy somehow, as if he shouldn't be in the same room as her. He broke her heart before she had the accident, and he wasn't sure she knew about the baby, which still lingered on his mind and cast a cloud over the excitement of Kayla's return. Everyone had been too happy to mention it.

"Kayla," he abruptly began right as her television show returned.

She turned her head slightly over to him with an indifferent look.

"I need to talk to you," he said.

"I'm listening."

He took a deep breath. "When you were in the coma, I knew I'd regret what I had done every single second of every day of my life. I still do, but I comfort myself thinking maybe, just maybe I can make it up to you."

Kayla looked down at her unmoving legs and kept her lips pursed together.

"Truth is, I love you and I always have. Nothing changed. I never meant I didn't love you when I left. It's just that…I'm screwed up. Prison wrecks a guy's mind, and I didn't want you to deal with that."

"You didn't ask me what I wanted to deal with," she said. "Instead you left me alone without even talking to me about it. Communication is a big deal, Russell. It's what kept us together all those years. And you failed to express yourself to me."

"I'm sorry!" he said. "I just knew you didn't want to. What you want and need are two different things –"

"What I *need* is Alexis's father. What I need is for us to be a close-knit family. What I need is your support after I gave it to you for seven years," she snapped.

"I know that now," Russell said softly. "I know that more than anything. I want and need you. This truly showed me."

"You know what? I'm pregnant. And I was prepared to have to deal with that all alone because of you. Do you know what I went through? But because you wanted nothing to do with me, I kept that to myself. Yes, I'm pregnant – is that going to make you run for the hills again?"

Russell fell silent. She thought she still had the baby – or she was just telling herself she still had it, clinging to the possibility, because no one had told her otherwise. So the task would fall to him at that uncomfortable moment in time.

"Kayla. You're not pregnant anymore."

Kayla twitched like she couldn't register that information. "What?" she asked sharply.

"We lost the baby."

Kayla let her head fall back on the pillow and rested her hands on her stomach. Sure enough, it was flatter than before. She looked at Russell imploringly. "Tell me that's not true," she whispered.

Russell looked back at her apologetically. "I'm sorry."

No more words needed to be spoken from that point onward. As Kayla visibly struggled with the Russell's abhorred news, she eventually gave in. Her face crumpled and her body was racking with sobs. Russell stood up and put his arm around her gently. Only he saw the nurse walking in. Once his eyes met the nurse's, they had a silent understanding. Kayla found out.

Dr. Leon sat in the hospital café for a while as he slowly sipped his ice tea after dinner. He could not decide whether he should stop by Kayla's room before going back to his apartment. While Kayla was in a coma, Dr. Leon perceived that it was his mission to help Kayla to regain consciousness. It seemed so easy to talk to her when she couldn't speak back. Now that Kayla had awakened, he was torn. He wanted to talk to her, yet he felt he was out of place, especially because he had met her family. He wondered whether her husband sensed anything; he had shown him an air of hostility when their eyes met.

Dr. Leon found his feet taking him into the direction of Kayla's room. It was automatic, robotic.

After all, I am moving thousands of miles away from here soon. What the heck, he said to himself.

CHAPTER 9

KAYLA
WHAT'S AHEAD?

Dr. Leon gently knocked at the door. Kayla was almost sitting up and casually watching a game show. "Mind if I come in?" he asked.

Kayla nodded with a wan smile. She was alone.

He pulled a chair over from the opposite wall and sat next to her bed.

Before he could open his mouth, Kayla whispered, "Thanks for everything."

Then there was a long silence. It was undeniable that there were many intimate and warm feelings between them. It felt natural for Kayla to just enjoy his presence, at least. But in that silence, Kayla knew she had to search for the right words—the words to define what they had. That is, until Dr. Leon spoke.

"I am concluding my residency training next week. I've gotten a fellowship position at University of Chicago Medical Center..." Dr. Leon began.

"Wow, that's impressive!" Kayla said.

"It's time to move back home, close to my family. I have been on the West Coast for ten years." Before he said anything he would regret (Kayla guessed), he stood up, pushed the chair back to where it was, and said, "Kayla, your waking up was the best gift I could receive before I leave."

That being said, and Kayla staying silent, he slowly moved toward the door.

"Wait," Kayla said. "Can we have a hug…like friends do?" She smiled warmly this time. He walked back over and returned a grin. They hugged.

As he rose from the hug, he moved his eyes toward the doorway. "Kayla, please take care," he said softly.

Dr. Leon slowly walked toward the door again. At that very moment, in the deepest part of her heart, Kayla secretly hoped that he would turn around and beg her, or at least propose to her, that she leave her marriage and run away with him.

He did turn around and looked intently at her. It seemed like he wanted to say something, yet was unable to come out with the right words. Kayla could almost see the gears turning in his brain, searching for the proper vocabulary or phrases as he struggled with what to say. With a tortured look, he then lowered his gaze and slightly shook his head. He looked up again and abruptly, yet passionately, said once more, "Kayla, please take care."

He turned on his heels immediately and left. A profound sadness struck Kayla as she stared at his figure disappearing into the hallway.

In the meantime, she would not understand why his voice sounded so familiar. It wasn't that she already knew him – his voice brought back memories that Kayla wasn't even sure were real or not. His voice intertwined with an ancient melody playing in a far-off corner of her brain, over and over and over. She knew the voice well…

◄—►

Kayla tried keeping it together—after all, she awoke even though it was possible she could stay comatose for the rest of her life, or "vegetative," as the doctors kept saying. But the baby was gone. Even though she was relatively early in her pregnancy, she felt like she lost a child she had forever. Length of time didn't abate the pain. Guilt swept over her.

If I had been paying more attention to that car…
If I didn't let Russell get me down…
If Russell hadn't done what he had done…

In the events after death, it was easy to play the blame game. Kayla didn't care that she had broken legs; that would heal itself in time, just like her arm and her face. Come what may—physical therapy, relearning to walk, whatever—she would never let the upcoming struggles get her down. When it came to her unborn child, though, she was inconsolable.

Veronica never spoke of it; she squeezed her arm and was more affectionate than normal while repeatedly declaring, "Let me know if there's anything I can do A-N-Y-T-H-I-N-G."

Alexis was happy as could be, unperturbed with her mother now awake and her father a less mysterious figure. She went back to school but visited Kayla after school everyday for about two hours, before Russell or Mrs. Mancini took her home for homework.

Russell walked in mid-morning, when everyone else was gone.

"I don't know why I wore this heavy sweatshirt," he mumbled. "It's getting warm outside."

"What day is it?" Kayla asked.

"April 13," Russell replied.

"Wow," she said. "I'm dizzy now…it's like I just magically lost a month and a half."

Russell settled himself in the chair beside her. "How are you doing?" he slowly asked. They needed no specifics on this. Kayla glanced at her uneaten tray of hospital food and released a shuddering sigh. She replied, "Not good. It's the worst thing to feel under the sun."

Russell saw the tears forming in her eyes and looked sorry he asked. He pulled a tissue from the box nearby and handed it to her. Kayla blew her nose and bit her lip in hopes of suppressing the tears. "I just can't talk about it without becoming a mess, but I almost *have* to talk about it," she said. She knew she couldn't bottle it up and pretend it never happened.

"I know what you're going through. That's needless to say," he said. He leaned closer and put his hand on her head, stroking her hair away so it wouldn't stick to her tear-streaked face. Kayla knew the only way she would get through any of this was with Russell. He was simply the only person who understood and fully shared her grief. When she looked up, she saw his ocean-colored eyes starting to overflow. Without a word, she grabbed his hand and squeezed it fiercely. He returned the act.

Together, as they watched the tears streaking down each other's face, they lessened the burden they carried. No one else in their circle knew the all-consuming depression that a miscarried child invoked.

"I have a proposition," Veronica said, clearing her throat as she, Alexis, and Russell sat around Kayla's bed one afternoon. "My neighbor is leaving next month. How about you guys take over their apartment lease? That way Alexis, Joycelyn, and Junior will all be close by, and I'll be a stone's throw away to help however I can."

Kayla saw Russell stiffen at the mention, as if he didn't want to return home to them.

Or maybe he feels awkward having left at all, said a kinder voice in Kayla's head.

"I can't exactly get all my things together and move," Kayla said. "I'd just oversee and be a pest."

"Robert has already offered to help. And we'll also put our kids to work to help out, too. Extra allowance," Veronica added.

"I could help," said Russell. "I'm able-bodied."

"Of course you will," said Veronica. "You'll be living there, too."

Kayla scoffed at how presumptuous Veronica was. No, she couldn't deny that's how it would be, but still...

"I guess since everyone's in on it but me, I can't say no," said Kayla. "The only reason I'm agreeing is that I'll be out of here by the end of the week."

"Awesome!" said Veronica. She looked as content as a cat after a belly rub. Kayla knew Veronica wanted to do her part after such a huge scare, but she hoped it was the right idea…

Was Russell *really* coming home? She glanced at his impassive face as he played cards with Alexis. If anything, maybe it was for her. She felt like she was starting from scratch, and the next steps in life were up in the air. Even if Russell tried to shake off his ties to Kayla, he couldn't lose his fatherhood.

On Kayla's last night in the hospital, everyone left her with a kiss before they would return and help before her discharge the next morning. She knew it was the most activity she will have been through ever since her accident, so she needed to rest. Russell, however, remained.

"I don't know about you, but I can't handle another second of the news," she said. "It's all so depressing."

"You took the words out of my mouth," he said. He rose up from the chair and started flipping through the channels using the button on the television. Kayla couldn't help but look at him instead of the options during his channel changing. Why was he there? Was he just being nice? Was it for Alexis? Did he really care? And if so, would he continue to declare he wasn't "good enough" for her?

"You know what, Animal Planet it is. It's mainly for background noise anyway," said Russell. As he turned around, he looked her in the eye as she was slightly leaned forward in bed, even though she had about four pillows behind her.

"Russell," she began, "what are we doing?"

His eyes darted back and forth. "Um, watching t—"

"No. In general. What the hell is gonna happen tomorrow when I'm discharged? Where do we go from here?"

She laughed bitterly, wondering why she'd have to even ask such a question. *How far we've come!* She thought.

Russell paused before sitting down in shock. "Well, I was coming back with you. Obviously."

"Not obviously," she said. "Before the...*accident*...well, we knew what the state of our relationship was. I don't even know what to expect anymore."

Russell leaned forward, staring at Kayla. "Even through all of that, I never felt any differently about you. Not once. Kayla, I love you."

Kayla felt like she should have been touched, but she felt too guarded to let the declaration penetrate her. She shook her head. "No. Your leaving me wasn't love. You might've thought you were being 'noble' or something, but you left me after I waited years for you. You left our daughter. You left me, pregnant..." Kayla broke off right there. The wound felt fresh and raw every time she brought it up.

In looking up at Russell and choking back sobs that threatened to erupt, she almost felt unfeeling. There, in his face, was pure devastation. He forgot to breathe for a moment as if she punched him in the stomach.

"Sorry." She sighed. "You know now."

"I wish I could take it back," he said, his voice breaking. "All of it. Everything from the past few years."

"Well, there's no use in that," Kayla said. "It all happened. I dealt with it. It's just your turn."

"That's the thing," he said in anguish. He jumped up from the chair and started pacing the room, not making eye contact. "I locked everything in. I wouldn't share the horror of everything to you because I thought you'd never understand. It made me upset that I couldn't relate to you. I thought I'd be doing you a favor by leaving because of that. But I never felt any different. Never. I loved you and still do. And I *know* it wouldn't happen again."

"But how do I know this is different?" Kayla asked softly. "You said you couldn't relate to me. How is it better now?"

"Because I know the meaning of for better or for worse. I know how much I need you. Thinking I'd lost you forever was worse than seven years in prison. By a long shot."

Kayla wasn't immune to what he was saying. She didn't want to turn him away, but the last thing she could ever deal with was being hurt again after all she had been through.

"Look, I don't want to lose you either. But I don't know if I can trust you. I don't know if this will work out! All I can think about is you leaving me and my thoughts afterward about raising two kids alone. Maybe we have changed. Maybe there's too much baggage," she said. She blinked back the tears that started burning her eyes yet again.

Russell stooped down and scooped her hand in his. With a squeeze he told her, "But I don't even care about what has already happened anymore. What's happened to me—to *us*—is hard, but...I now know the only way to get past it is through you. The last thing I should have done was push you away. I guess I understand if you don't want me around, but I'd love to be around to help you through, just as you wanted to help me."

Kayla stayed silent, still furiously blinking to withhold her tears.

"Kayla, I love you. I hope you know that."

Clearing her throat, she replied, "I know. I love you, too. We have a lot to heal from, between the two of us. I guess it doesn't hurt to try, together."

She squeezed his hand in return. They both smiled tearfully, lingering in the moment. Kayla knew, come what may, she loved him and didn't foresee that changing anytime soon. She just hoped that it could work—for her sake and the family's.

CHAPTER 10

FORWARD THINKING

As soon as Kayla was discharged and arrived back home, everything was surreal. Russell and Robert had to team up and lift her off of the wheelchair inside, and Veronica shouted orders. Then Kayla saw everything: the worn couch, the kitchen where she and Russell fought, and the table in the breakfast nook, where she sat, nauseous, before the accident. They were back where they left off, but only in theory.

Robert and Russell settled her onto the couch, Russell stroking her shoulder before letting go. When Veronica walked in, she pushed her sunglasses onto her forehead, holding back her espresso-brown bangs. "Kay, do you want anything to drink after all that moving? Another pillow?"

"Water and yes, two. I'm really getting used to this treatment, by the way," said Kayla with a small smirk. "I'll be a spoiled brat by the end."

"Sadly, I don't even mind," said Veronica, rushing to the kitchen to fill up a glass of water. "Let's just hope your daughter doesn't mind once she and Mrs. Mancini come over."

While Kayla was home, she felt engulfed by lots of people and lots of love. Robert helped Russell bring the wheelchair back in and joked "that thing is heavier than you." Mrs. Mancini came over with a baked ziti and Alexis, who just got back from soccer practice.

"It's easy! You just toss it in the microwave and add some extra Parmesan cheese. Even Alexis has done it."

"I know how to microwave stuff," she said with an eye roll.

After that, the others left, leaving the three alone. With Alexis around, it wasn't too awkward, but even still, Kayla had bigger fish to fry: physical therapy.

Once the day came, Russell drove her in the rickety car he'd had since before he was arrested. Each bump, speedy acceleration, and slamming on the breaks aggravated her old rib injuries.

"I hope this isn't a sign of the pain to come," Kayla said with a groan. She rested her forehead against the cool glass of the window and enviously watched long-legged, California-tanned women striding down the pavement.

"Well, it's therapy. So shouldn't it be therapeutic?" Russell gave her a small smile.

"I hope there's a masseuse involved," she replied.

Once they pulled up, Russell ran around to the back of the car and unfolded Kayla's wheelchair. Wrapping her arm around his neck, he gently lowered her in. The simple act of his driving her there made her heart swell with gratitude.

"I really don't know how I'd do this without you," she said. "I guess I'd crawl here."

Russell grinned. "Glad to have a purpose."

The first session of physical therapy went smoothly. Much of the time was spent assessing her limitations and discussing her history. The physical therapist, Mr. Shin, who was under the supervision of Dr. Jennus, bent her knee joint repeatedly.

"Eventually, we're going to move you to that treadmill," he pointed to the contraption that would strap her in. "But not for a while yet." His face crinkled into a reassuring smile.

Over time, the sessions became harder and harder. She left one session having broken out into a sweat and feeling exhausted and defeated afterward. During the ride home, she felt even more bitter seeing couples taking a stroll out by the bay, women jogging, kids skateboarding, and an older gentleman walking his fluffy chow-chow.

"Want me to stop for anything?" Russell ventured cautiously. Kayla lifted her cheek from her fist. "No."

"Are you sure? I'll pay—"

"What, with your mom's money?"

At Russell's crestfallen face, Kayla eased up. "Sorry. I just don't know how I'm going to get back to how I was. I hate this!"

"That was below the belt, Kayla." Russell stared straight ahead, gripping the steering wheel.

Oh, great, she thought. *Now I've made him depressed, too.*

What would take another couple days to express to Russell was that Kayla missed independence. She was used to doing everything on her own—everything. She had always managed school, work, and childrearing all alone. Now she couldn't do any of those things. Having Russell around helping her was an abrupt change.

"I just don't know how to rely on someone else," she said in bed the next night. "This is frustrating anyway, but especially because I've gotten to be a control freak."

Russell stared at the ceiling looked visibly miffed anyway, but he said he'd put it behind him.

Each day, morose minutes slowly dripped into an anxious hour. Hours trickled by. There was only so much television Kayla could watch and food for her family to fetch before she drove herself crazy.

"I've got cabin fever," she muttered to Alexis. "When you run in soccer, run for the both of us."

"It sounds okay to lay around all day," Alexis said cheerfully. "No school!"

That's what made Kayla the most anxious – not school, but work. Someone needed to make money around there. They were moving into the apartment by Veronica's the next week, and she was concerned that if she didn't get well fast enough, she'd lose her job and would be unable to afford it. In government housing, it wasn't an issue. She couldn't help but bite her nails at the thought.

"That's hogwash," Breeana said when Kayla brought up her job fears during their next Skype date. Russell had moved the computer over to Kayla so she could talk to her friend and stay occupied. "Getting hit by a car and being in a coma is a huge deal! Don't blame yourself for anything. It would get the best of us down."

Kayla's lip nevertheless managed to quiver.

"Come on," Breeana said gently. "I'm just glad you're around. I didn't get the news until you were already waking up. I thought you had either lost Internet or decided not to keep in touch anymore. But your excuse trumps all that."

"Sorry," Kayla said. "Everyone was too worried to remember."

"Everyone forgetting me – my worst fear," said Breeana facetiously.

"I guess you should come back to the United States for awhile."

Breeana's eyes twinkled with glee, on the brink of exciting news. Kayla recognized it. "Alright, out with it!" she said.

"Well, maybe you'll have an opportunity to come here in the near-ish future," Breeana said.

Kayla pointed down to her lower half. "Can't. I'm crippled. I got some bum legs."

"It wouldn't be for a while. I'm talking a year or a year and a half."

"Now you're just being mean. What's the news?"

Breeana slowly lifted her left hand and revealed a huge round-cut diamond with a halo of smaller diamonds around it. It was a pristine white gold.

Kayla gasped. "I know what that means! Congratulations!"

They both squealed at the sight of the dazzling rock on her finger as it caught the light.

"So gimme all the details," Kayla said. As usual, hearing Breeana's stories took Kayla to another world where wine, relaxation, city lights, and carefree living were the norm. She let herself be transported there for a minute.

Breeana explained every painstaking detail about Stefan's proposal—in short, he planned a scavenger hunt around their favorite Paris destinations, giving her clues on where to go for the next step. At the very end, he played guitar at a café with the Eiffel Tower in view before dropping on one knee and proposing to her.

"That's so romantic I feel like I'll throw up," said Kayla jokingly.

"I imagined you'd say something like that!" said Breeana with a deep belly laugh, making her ebony curls bounce. "But seriously. You're my maid of honor. I couldn't imagine that you wouldn't be there – it simply isn't an option."

Kayla could see her eyes widening in the corner of the screen.

"Well, as long as there's time to save up…"

"I would help you anyway," Breeana interrupted. "Don't worry."

Kayla strummed her fingers on the keys. "Well, hopefully it won't come to that. Just keep me updated on the day."

The conversation lifted Kayla's spirits considerably. Instead of feeling like she was typing through thick fog, she energetically started web surfing pictures of Paris. Images of the multicolored gardens of Versailles among the long and glittering fountains, the bloody history of fortress of the Bastille, and the treasure trove of art in the Louvre all set Kayla's heart racing. She imagined herself strolling through the cobblestone streets, chomping into a baguette, and listening to a man playing the accordion in a beret.

But therein lay the problem: the *strolling* part.

"I need to get past being an invalid," Kayla moaned. The dark feelings of frustration and gloom settled over her like toxic gas once again.

When Kayla told Russell about Breeana's wedding while they lay in bed that night, he worried about their ability to do go. He continued shaking his head throughout her excited chatter, much to Kayla's annoyance. Before long, he turned over so all Kayla could see was the dark, curved outline of his back.

"I just don't know," he said shortly.

Kayla thought steam would blow from her ears. "Breeana said she'd help. It means everything to her for me to go. That is, if I can *ever* walk again!"

"Of course you will walk again!" said Russell. "Don't think like that."

Kayla thought about Russell's ability to give encouragement, but his inability to receive it. She already knew his thoughts ventured back to his feeling useless again. Maybe there was more to his fear about the affordability of a Paris trip.

Kayla spoke gently. "I know you feel useful with me like this, but I hate it. I hope that, once I gain back my independence, you'll believe in your *own* ability to walk."

Sliding her hand around his torso, she held him close, Russell covered her hand with his until they fell asleep.

CHAPTER 11

WALKING LESSONS
FOR TWO

Kayla was sitting in the midst of frenzied scurrying. Veronica swooped past her; Alexis clonked by with a box of old toys. Russell's and Robert's biceps bulged as they put their backs into moving the heavy arm chair. Joycelyn and Robert Jr. tossed assorted odds and ends into boxes. The world was moving around as Kayla was still, and she hated it.

"I feel useless," she mumbled to Veronica.

"Don't. Savor it. You get to shout orders instead!" Veronica replied.

Momentarily Kayla forgot about the conversation, knowing she needed to take one lingering glance around the trailer. Though dirty and cramped, it was her first official home. When Veronica wheeled Kayla outside toward the car, she realized she was being wheeled away from the trailer one last time.

"Hold on," she instructed her older sister. So many memories were tucked away in that trailer – mostly bad, but still, the trailer was her sanctuary for many lonely years. She felt tugged between the car to her new future and the trailer, beside which Dorothy now stood. She had her hands folded in front of her skirt, which had aqua, black, white, and pink geometrical patterns on it. Looking up, Kayla saw Dorothy give a sad smile.

"You didn't think you were going to leave without saying good-bye, did ya?" asked Dorothy. "I'm hurt."

Kayla crossed her arms. "Now, Dorothy, you know this move doesn't mean a thing. You can still come over and visit whenever you want. I can assure you that once I'm moving I'll be dropping by like old times."

"You'd best." Dorothy walked over, bent down, and gave Kayla a big hug.

"Take care," she whispered to Kayla. "Never forget to give me updates please."

"You got it."

After they settled into their new apartment, Alexis's eyes were the size of Frisbees. "There's so much space!" she said. Getting a running start, she pranced around the empty space of the living room. "We should leave this as a gymnastics area! A play room!"

"And that would be a huge waste of space," replied Kayla. "Enjoy this while it lasts."

The grueling moving day continued, and Kayla continued sitting in the wheelchair and feeling helpless. Seeing the sweat pouring down the others' faces, she decided to be the self-proclaimed "water girl" and rolled to the sink to fill a pitcher.

"Here you go," she said, handing Russell a glass while he wiped the back of his hand across his forehead. "I bet this is perfect timing after lifting the breakfast table up."

"That's not so bad. It's just doing it over and over that makes it hard. Endurance."

"Well, to be honest, I'm jealous," Kayla said. "I'm sitting here watching you do all the work."

"Now you know how I feel," he said. Unsmiling, he walked back downstairs to get more items.

She lifted her eyebrows. *That negativity drives me insane,* she thought, shaking her head. Right when she thought they were doing okay, Russell was sinking back into depression once again. It all began with the mention of Paris. Now that Kayla was improving in physical therapy, she imagined Russell was worried he'd become obsolete again.

Soon Kayla was able to walk on crutches and go to work – not as long as before, and doing mostly sit-down duties – but at least it was bringing some money back in. Once Kayla could work, Russell started his slump back into sitting on the couch all day, sleeping for hours on end, and, Kayla suspected, becoming nervous at his own job prospects.

All the while, images of miscarried children haunted her dreams.

Thankfully, he never said no to cooking. Kayla remembered when Alexis was just born, Russell had said, "I love you, but *I'll* do the cooking from now on," which was his tactful way of saying Kayla's food went down like rocks and glue. They had laughed, and Kayla said she wouldn't mind doing the eating while Russell did the cooking. He could throw together a delicious pizza on a tortilla like it was nothing. The one ray of light in their otherwise cloudy world was that still, as Kayla was recovering, Russell could still make a pizza on a tortilla. The crispy, thin "crust" balanced out the gooey cheese and the olive oil seasoning spread perfectly.

Even if Kayla felt too depressed for words, or Russell was clearly concerned about getting back into the world, Kayla looked forward to dinner – a time period where he reigned in the kitchen once again after becoming reacquainted with it, forgetting his troubles. When Kayla looked down at his handiwork, she felt the same way.

But it was not enough.

Wondering who Kayla could speak to – she desperately hoped it could be somebody unbiased – she rummaged through her brain. Looking at the ankle she had broken the previous year, a light bulb popped over her head. She picked up her cell phone and dialed the number listed on the website.

"Hi Dr. Chen. It's Kayla Mancini…I'm doing well, thanks. I was wondering if we could meet one day. I need some advice."

Riding the bus was no easy feat with crutches and crowds. Rubbing her underarms once she sat down, she hoped she didn't have blisters. Once the famous green sign came into view, she eagerly picked up her purse and her crutches.

Dr. Chen waited outside on the Starbucks patio, the end-of-July warm breeze gently tossing her shiny, brown hair.

When Kayla saw her, Dr. Chen waved and leaned forward on her elbows. "Hello!" she said.

"Want to be a gentleman and open the door for me so I can grab some coffee?" said Kayla lightheartedly.

"Of course," said Dr. Chen. They walked inside to stand in line and exchanged small talk. Kayla didn't know how coffee would be with her nervous disposition lately, but she yearned for the rich, roasted flavor to add some joy to the lackluster conversation she was about to have.

Dr. Chen graciously carried Kayla's cup outside back on the patio and pulled out her chair so Kayla wouldn't have to.

"Thank you," Kayla said.

"What did you want to see me for?" she asked. Her warm smile encouraged Kayla to open up.

"Well, I'm considering going back to school to pursue my masters degree..."

Strangely, Dr. Chen's smile fell into a horizontal line. She only nodded slightly.

Kayla sensed Dr. Chen's concern. "What do you think?"

"Kayla, there is never anything wrong with attaining a higher education."

Somehow, Kayla wasn't convinced. "Well, I checked online. I understand that I need to take the GRE before applying for graduate school. I know I can do it."

Dr. Chen took a sip of her ginger green tea and looked thoughtful. Kayla knew her perceptive advisor could feel her lack of confidence. She confirmed it by saying, "Kayla, do you mind if I ask you something personal?"

"Not at all."

"Do you think you are going 'back to school' as an escape?"

Kayla looked at her blankly, gripping the piping hot coffee cup.

"Because," Dr. Chen continued, "I remember how anxious you were to be finished with your education. Have these few months changed that? Tell me, though, physical limitations aside, what do you really want deep down in your heart? What immediately comes to mind?"

Somehow, the memories of her own fearful, insecure childhood flashed through her mind. Her mother leaving, not knowing her father...and then Kayla thought about seeing Alexis's round, cherub face for the first time. She imagined Alexis's situation if Kayla hadn't made it through the coma. Her chest tightened. Without hesitation, Kayla replied, "I want to do all I possibly can to provide a safe, secure, and stable life for my child. Ironically, Alexis has missed some of it the past several years. I want to make sure I can compensate for that for the rest of her childhood."

Dr. Chen's knowing eyes penetrated into Kayla's mind. She sipped her tea yet again before asking, "How can you make that happen?"

Barely audible, Kayla replied, "I really need to work on my marriage...I thought once Russell came home everything would be fine. But it turned out so much harder than I thought..."

"I know what you mean. Just remember what you really want. Repeat your want over and over and over again, and then work toward it. This way you will not be regretful in the future." Dr. Chen smiled reassuringly. "The rest is up to you. Sometimes people need to retrace their steps and start from scratch for a new, positive path."

"Kayla, marriage is very hard work. There is no perfect marriage just like there are no perfect people! You are not alone. Don't give up!" Dr. Chen added before they departed. Kayla sucked on that thought as she walked away.

Lord knows there's no perfect person out there, and imperfect people can't have a perfect marriage.

The sun seemed to shine just a little brighter as she crutched out of the coffee shop.

That night, after Alexis went to bed, Kayla asked Russell if they could talk. They sat at the old table from the trailer, directly across from one another. Kayla made them tea, feeling that after her heart-to-heart with Dr. Chen, it would help to have a distraction.

"Let's cut to the chase," Kayla said. "I love you. You love me. But we just don't know if this marriage is going to work out."

Russell looked at her in surprise. "Well, yes, I love you. But…"

"This is a tell-all conversation. We're going to be honest. No more elephant in the room. Russell, those are my thoughts. We love each other but are worried this marriage won't work."

Russell dipped the tea bag in and out of the mug. "I suppose so," he muttered. Kayla looked at him with raised eyebrows. "Okay, you're right," he conceded.

"I knew it. But here's the thing: whenever we stop worrying about the marriage, we do just fine. Whenever we start worrying about our capabilities, the details, what we lost…" Kayla gulped back tears at the mention of the miscarriage. "…etc, we fall into negativity and take it out on each other. Enough with the details! It doesn't matter how good or bad you think you are. *I* think you're the greatest man I've ever met. And it only matters what I think of you."

Kayla grabbed his hand before she continued. "Will you support me through physical therapy? Can I support you back to a life? Can we support each other through grief, and can we just start over on a new life together?"

Russell's eyes became bloodshot as he nodded slowly. "I can't say no to that speech," he said with weak laughter. "I love you."

"Good. Because I love you. We need each other at our best." Kayla blinked back tears.

At that moment, all the grief from their loss, from the months together, from the *years* apart, flooded forward. Russell pushed back his chair. He went to Kayla's side of the table, stooping down and picking her up. She wrapped his arms around his neck and held him close.

They had a lot to cope with and plenty of struggles to come. That was no mistake. But the only way they would surpass the troubles was if they ran for it head on, holding each other's hand.

For the first time in months, Kayla felt equipped to deal with what was ahead of them. Especially because, after their tearful embrace, she found herself standing on her own two feet.

Standing tall at last.

CHAPTER 12

WHAT GOES DOWN MUST COME UP

Six months after Kayla's accident, and she was making great strides in physical therapy—literally. Leaning on the handlebars on the treadmill, she could take slow, cautious steps. Unfortunately, months of lying and sitting down weakened her significantly, so even a short walk left her breathless. Russell watched on proudly as she took a four-minute walk.

"Phew," she said. "I will never take walking for granted again. Running is unthinkable, and marathon runners just sound unrealistic."

Russell laughed and handed her a towel. "They always sounded unrealistic to you," he said.

Mr. Shin called it a day while congratulating her on her progress. "It shouldn't be long now," he said. "Just don't try to do too much at once. Rome wasn't built in a day."

"Thank you, I will never be a couch potato when it's over," she said.

With more and more sessions, Kayla was learning to walk again. In the meantime, though, Russell took care of the house. When she made particularly good progress, Russell cooked up some pasta—what he called a twist on his mother's kitchen special.

"I tried adding some of the canned vegetables that have been sitting around," he said. "So I don't know how it tastes. I need to go get some fresh vegetables."

Kayla twirled the noodles around her fork and smiled. "This tastes like your best, if you ask me. It's a perfect victory dinner."

Russell and Kayla sat at the table and touched their garlic bread together in a toast. "To the taste of victory," said Kayla with a smile. "And that I can one day walk off all your Italian food."

Russell looked high and low for a job but with no success. He submitted applications to little retail stores, home improvement warehouses, and even fast food. While Alexis was at school, Kayla insisted upon coming when she could to support him, especially if he was only dropping off an application. The amount of time it took to quickly go inside was the perfect amount of walking practice for her. She worked four days of ten-hour shifts with three days off weekly.

Together, they walked up to a sports clothing store. "This seems like your kind of place," said Kayla, giving Russell a playful nudge. "Mention you're a former swimmer!"

While inside, it was mainly empty because it was a Monday morning—aside from a manager with wide shoulders offset by a lean waist. He wore a royal blue dry-fit shirt and was putting new sweatshirts on hangers.

"Hey there!" the manager shot them a grin. "How can I help ya?"

"I have an application," Russell announced. Kayla could tell he was trying to appear confident as he stood tall and rolled his shoulders back.

"Well that's an answered prayer. We could really use somebody," the extroverted manager said. "If you could just hand that to me, we will see what we can do."

Russell extended it to him and the manager excitedly snatched it. As his eyes scanned along Russell's experience, he said, "Quite a gap in experience, there. What, seven years?"

Russell remained silent, staring down at the checkout counter. Every manager was deterred by that – but that was nothing compared to what they would see on his record.

"Oh," the manager said, his eyes widening at what was undoubtedly Russell's criminal history. Kayla's heart sank as the manager looked up. "Well thanks for your application. I will be in touch."

Russell smiled as if unperturbed and firmly shook the manager's hand, trying not to pay attention to the fact the broad man was clearly disenchanted with the idea of hiring him.

On their way out, Kayla leaned on him. "Somewhere else," Kayla said confidently. "Who would wanna work for that meathead, anyway?"

Russell let out a disheartened sigh. "On with the search."

Unfortunately it did not get easier. When Russell called back for his application status, they didn't answer or return his calls. If they actually picked up, they said they had since "reviewed applications that more closely fit the needs" of their workplace. Fast food denied him, and one manager even said, "We don't need your kind here."

For months Russell looked, only to return home downtrodden. Kayla was the breadwinner as she continued working at the neonatal unit in the hospital. He felt frustrated and "castrated," as Kayla said. "You feel like you need to provide for us because you're a man. But don't be too prideful. It's not the 1950s." She tried to be lighthearted, but she knew when to refrain. She saw how Russell's head slumped a little lower after each failed attempt. Though he tried to stand tall, she saw his insecure shuffle slowly return. Well, he helped her take her first steps, and she was more than ready to return the favor.

"I know, I know it will take time," he said. "But I need to be useful. I'm a stay at home dad…"

"Consider it bonding time with Alexis until your dream job comes along." Kayla kissed his cheek and reassured him something would come along. "We know better than anybody that 'nothing worth having in life comes easy.'"

Russell gave her a small smile before kissing her on the cheek. As many negative emotions that were surely swirling around him, at least he wasn't "doom and gloom" anymore, to Kayla's relief. Soon, he would even be inspired.

One day, Russell stopped by a food truck to get something to eat while returning home from a walk down to the bay for more job hunting around the retail shopping strip. The truck boasted some of the best smoked and fried chicken around along with "jaw-dropping" sauce, a family recipe handed down over the generations. As he dug into his pockets and withdrew some cash, an idea dawned on him, blinding him to everything else. He imagined his own pristine white truck splattered with eye-catching paint and lined with locals...

"Hey, you gonna take your food?" The food truck employee asked.

Russell blinked rapidly as he came back to reality. "Oh yeah. Thanks." He dropped the coins with a little clatter on the counter and grabbed his fried chicken.

When he was home, he couldn't help but glance at the computer with an itch to investigate the food truck business. But he was too busy sketching. On a sheet of printer paper, he roughly outlined the silhouette of a van and wrote a list of different names off to the side.

"Russell's Roma Cuisine."

"Rusty's Real Italian."

No matter how silly the name seemed, he scrawled it down beside the van. Failing to see that Kayla arrived to the apartment and slumped in the chair beside him, she shouted boo. Only then did he glance up; he was a man on a mission.

"What's going on here? Taking art lessons?" she asked, taking her purse off her shoulder and placing it by the foot of the couch.

Russell grinned, too excited to be bashful. He stuck the pencil behind his ear and turned to her. "Maybe it needs work," he said. "But I had an idea..."

With that, Russell spoke animatedly about his idea, showing Kayla the research he gathered so far, and let her see the sketches of his vision. He spoke with his hands, made great eye contact, and his face frequently cracked into a smile. He was beginning to feel relevant again, and it felt sweet.

"Making my own business is a lot easier than getting hired," he said energetically. "With *my* record."

"You cook all the time anyway. I wonder how Alexis and I ate for the past seven years."

"We held our breaths and tried not to taste it," shouted Alexis from the hallway.

"You're grounded!" said Kayla jokingly. "But no, really – that's a great idea. Start your own business. Be your own boss. You have some delicious Italian recipes in your family and I for one would buy it."

"You mean it?"

"Absolutely. You can throw together anything and make it taste like a masterpiece." Kayla wrapped her hands around his. "Let's get cooking."

CHAPTER 13

NOSEDIVE! AGAIN?

With Kayla's support, Russell planned his food truck business thoroughly. It would serve Italian food, created from his own recipes for sauces and meatballs; plus he created his own version of mini cheesecakes. He shopped for the best quality ingredients, waking up early in the morning to taste test the food. Everything was made from scratch. He even planted seeds to grow his own basil and oregano in the small containers outside, on the balcony of their apartment.

Whenever Kayla returned from work, an array of scents would waft toward her nostrils. Her eyes twinkled as she saw Russell stirring something aromatic and red in a pot.

"Taste this," he offered, zooming toward her with a wooden spoon as if she were an infant and the spoon were the airplane.

Kayla carefully took a bite, trying to move her tongue out of the way so it wouldn't get scalded. After a careful nibble, her eyes widened. "Wow, that is good." She moved past Russell and glanced in the pot. It was thick without being chunky, like a smoothie, but there were green flecks of homegrown spices in it.

"It's my marinara sauce," Russell said proudly.

"It looks and tastes complex enough to be a stew," she said. "I would eat spoonfuls of it alone!"

Each day there was a new treat to taste. As Russell accumulated marketable recipes, his mood soared sky-high. He didn't mind going to the bank to take out a loan one bit – an act that would have stressed him or anyone else out immensely prior to his recent success.

One night, they hosted a housewarming at their apartment to celebrate Kayla's ability to walk, and so Russell could give samples of his latest recipes. As Kayla reminded Alexis to wash her hair, Russell was arranging his mini cheesecakes on a platter.

"Those look cute," said Kayla. Russell smiled and said, "Wait until you see what else I do."

Kayla rested her elbows on the counter as she saw Russell drizzle melted dark chocolate on a plump pair of raspberries atop each cheesecake. It looked positively seductive. Next, Russell stuck toothpicks into individual meatballs and stuck them in mini martini glasses with his marinara sauce inside.

"Voila, meatball martini," he said with a chuckle.

That night, as Dorothy, Veronica and Robert, their kids, Russell's parents, and any lingering high school friends came over, Russell's creations were the talk of the night. Dorothy bit into a meatball and closed her eyes.

"Oh my word! Someone get me a whole plate of these," she said. Kayla grinned and said, "There's plenty more where that came from. Russell has been making them almost every other day."

"She doesn't need to taste the mess-ups," Russell said with a bashful smile. "But you can anticipate the opening of my food truck."

That's when he broke the news. Dorothy put her hand on her hip and demanded to know which truck.

"It's a work in progress," Russell said mysteriously. "But I will keep you all updated."

That's when Veronica raised her glass. "To my sister and her husband. They're here and healthy once again."

Kayla lifted her fizzy drink and glanced over the bubbles at her husband, her heart bursting with pride. She hoped against all odds, he wouldn't have to face another disappointment again for a long while.

The night was as close to perfect as could be. Upbeat music filled their apartment, they ate good food, and best of all, Kayla showcased her walking once again. She would have worn heels to mark the occasion, but she went with pearl-colored kitten heels because she was never much of a stiletto person anyway, much preferring comfort over style.

◂—←—→—▸

After finding a good location, catered toward a lot of the blue-collar workers in the area, Russell's food truck was on the market. He painted it as to attract customers and promised free samples to the first newcomers. Kayla held her camera to her chest and told him to stand in front of it so she could snap a photo. With his arms crossed in front of his chest, Russell smiled, satisfied, in front of the only endeavor he had ever been proud of. Kayla proudly uploaded the photo to her Facebook that night.

Russell built up steady patrons and new customers spread via word of mouth. He was polite and delightful to customers.

He made his food look, smell, and taste delicious while being portable for people to take to go. Kayla couldn't have been prouder, glad that an entrepreneurial spirit and zeal for work replaced Russell's previous dejection and lost mentality. She helped out whenever she could on her days off.

A few months of success went by, bringing the family closer together than ever before. Money came in from both Kayla and Russell. Blissfully, both were comfortable with where they were and what they were doing. Even less of a concern was Breeana's wedding.

"We're having a longer engagement," she announced via Skype. "We're now shooting for next spring or summer."

"Why's that?" asked Kayla.

"Well, Dad's health hasn't been the best," Breeana began, referring to her father's heart surgery he had only a month before. In spite of her earlier concerns, he was pulling through. Still, though, she wanted to give him sufficient time to recover and strengthen before a trip to Europe.

"And anyway," she continued, "Stefan and I want to travel first. It's such a great time of life, Kayla, and I intend to soak in every minute of my engagement."

I wouldn't know, Kayla thought, but she felt she understood. "Of course. And after Russell starting up his business, this will give us sufficient time to save."

Life, Kayla pondered after their conversation. *If it's too good to be true, it can't be, right? But it is.*

She allowed herself to give into daydreams of Paris – she and Russell holding hands along the Seine, seeing the

Eiffel Tower on the orange and purple dusk horizon...two successful people, fully enjoying the labors of years past.

Russell stumbled inside their home, running his hands through his hair repeatedly, looking like he'd just witnessed a murder or ghost. Kayla scooted back her chair from the table and ran over to him.

"You look spooked, what the hell just happened?" Kayla asked. Russell was pacing around in circles and all but hyperventilating.

"Oh my god, sit down. I can't even...I can't believe..."

"I think you're the one who needs to sit down," Kayla said. "I'll bring you some water, try and relax."

Ignoring the immediate sinking feeling in her stomach, Kayla breathed deeply while filling the cup. She sat beside Russell, handed it to him, and calmly asked, "Okay, let's talk. What happened?"

Russell rested his face in his hands and began to rub his eyes. "A group of troublemakers came over today," he muttered. "They demanded food without paying. I said, 'Absolutely not.' I tried to hold my ground. Next thing I knew they were hopping onto the truck, got in the back, and started destroying everything, pillaging it of all the food. I was worried it would get physical. I shouted at them to get the hell out, I'd call the cops, etc. When I grabbed my cell phone, they just grabbed whatever they could and stormed out." Russell exhaled sharply, having said almost everything in one swift breath.

Kayla sat back in her chair, eyes darting side to side. For some reason the startling story he just told her didn't register. "So…wait. What happened to the truck?" she asked slowly.

"I drove the truck away before the police could show up. My truck is ruined."

Russell was simply shell shocked, just as unable to process the incident as Kayla was. Either that, or he had intermittent angst and shouts of, "What will I do?"

Once the reality settled into Kayla's mind, she knew the only way to comfort Russell was to stay calm herself.

"Let me call the insurance company. Russ, it will not be a big loss. Remember the lender insisted for us to get a business owner's policy when we applied for the business loan? Just stay right there, they may want to ask you in person about the details of the event." She filled him another glass of cold water, which he accepted in relief momentarily.

Kayla quickly found the insurance package, which she kept in the top drawer of her dresser. She dialed the number on the paper inside the package. It would be a hassle and prolonged process to deal with the insurance company, but that was the only way for them to claim the financial loss – *but not the heartache and the shattered dreams!*

When Kayla heard the door unlock later that afternoon, she ran over to answer it, immediately pulling Alexis aside.

Come on, she mouthed, pulling her into her daughter's bedroom. Alexis didn't even take her book bag off.

"What happened?" she asked, nervously messing with the elastic hair tie on her wrist.

"Your father has had an awful, awful day. I wanted to warn you before you saw his state."

"How?"

Kayla told Alexis the minimum amount of details – that the truck was robbed – but that was enough. Alexis, now in middle school, was a quiet girl and a daddy's girl. She said nothing. But when she left the room, she gave him a hug since he appeared to need it.

Later that night, Kayla and Russell spoke at the dinner table while Alexis was asleep, per usual.

"You can't let this deter you," Kayla said, clasping his hand in hers. "I don't even care if it's too early to say that, but you will find something else."

Russell sat in stoic silence. "I don't know," he said shortly.

"You know…you really do show great promise in cooking. There's no reason why that talent and passion shouldn't power you through to something else."

"I can't even imagine setting my sights on something else after all I've done to make the truck happen," he said in a dejected tone.

Kayla nodded, knowing that her support was the best help she could give at that moment. When words failed, touch helped. She held onto his hand all through the night, even as they were falling asleep.

As difficult as it was to accept the fate of the food truck, Kayla and Russell were accustomed to setbacks; they were the norm, as Kayla said. Thankfully, they had been learning about the way each other coped best through that whole time. Kayla learned when to stay silent, not lending any jocularity when unnecessary, and Russell was coping better with his insecurities. In any case, their sustenance was holding onto each other.

One day a couple months later, Kayla was watching television while she paid the bills. That's when a commercial popped up advertising a culinary institution. Students in crisp white chef uniforms smiled at the camera as the voiceover advertised "the latest methods and technologies" and "individual support in a team setting."

Kayla's hand, still holding a pen, froze in midair. She could almost hear the gears clicking in her head. "Bingo," she said aloud. With that epiphany she ran into their bathroom, where Russell had just showered.

"What about going to culinary school?" she asked breathlessly.

Russell pulled a shirt over his head and looked at her through the slightly steamed mirror. "Go on," he said.

"I am sure with the official training, you will excel in this area. You have the genes for it! Why not try it? I just saw a commercial and hey, why not?"

His countenance lit up slightly. "It's a possibility. But the job market, especially with my limitations, doesn't sound too appealing right now..."

"We will talk about it, but who knows...maybe that will boost you to where you need to be."

Kayla let him digest the idea and tried to contain her excitement over it in the meantime.

A couple weeks passed, and Russell still seemed to be recovering, but he did appear more thoughtful. Kayla found him surfing the web and taking Alexis out more like in old times. She just couldn't help but wonder if he'd give in...

"Hey. Where are you headed?" asked Kayla one evening as Russell rose from the couch.

"You'll see," he said enigmatically.

Kayla pouted. "I do not like surprises."

Russell turned back around with a smirk and walked out the door. Naturally Kayla couldn't get it out of her mind, but it didn't prevent her from taking a nap – work had been busy that morning, and that was an understatement.

What Kayla awoke to was Russell's gentle nudging. As Kayla's eyes adjusted to the bedside lamp he had turned on, she turned her attention to the sheet of paper in his hand.

"Congratulations! You have been accepted to the Culinary Institute..."

That's all she needed to hear. Wrapping her arms around his neck, she held him close.

"I'm so proud of you."

CHAPTER 14

WHAT'S COOKING?

Russell hoped square one this time around would do the trick. While he was still in the school, he submitted his various recipes to local culinary competitions and won several prizes. He completed his culinary training with high marks. Russell was not only good at creating delicious and complex flavors, but also with artistic presentation. Making delicacies like crème brulée and baked halibut late at night, Kayla and Alexis were both willing taste testers. While Russell experienced moments of insecurity, he delved into his passion as Kayla backed him up. That was his escape from his haunting past.

When Russell came home, it wasn't unusual for him to have a ribbon, a check, and a chest puffed out in pride. The girls scrambled off the couch excitedly.

"You're looking at the first-prize winner of my class's cook-off."

"For what?" Alexis asked.

"My sorbet," he replied.

"How about you make some for us for dessert tonight?" said Kayla with a wink.

After winning local competitions, he started moving on up to the bigger contests with the bigger prizes. Winning those would guarantee his future as a formidable chef. Kayla saw how he dove into the preparations and excitement of it, but she also saw a hint of tenseness. She hoped that he could give into unbridled confidence, running into the new era of his life fearlessly.

Russell stood in the convention center for the national culinary competition, awash with chattering so that all he could hear was white noise with the intermittent echo of the loudspeaker. Russell was one of the ten finalists to compete in the national culinary competition. Not only had the cash prize increased dramatically this year due to the generous sponsorships, but also the winner would go to the International Culinary Competition and receive endorsements. The entire competition was aired live at the network TV channel, which made all the contestants even more nervous.

This year's judges were known for being critical not only regarding taste but preparation and presentation. They sampled each dish, staring down their beak-like noses as if ready to claw the other judges and fly away with the most prized tastes.

Across the parking lot on the way in, Russell saw his "rival" from class, Paul. They were both always at the top of their game while having completely opposing tastes—literally. Both tirelessly competitive, they kept each other at the edges of their seats.

When Russell stepped inside and kissed Alexis and Kayla before they took their seats, Paul marched over like a cop ready to bust an underage party.

"So how's it going, Mancini?" he casually asked.

"Going well, Paul. I feel confident about my dishes."

Paul raised his eyebrows and licked his lips like he was onto something. "I wonder how the judges would feel if they knew your past. Hmm, what do you think?"

Russell's mouth dried. He felt like his blood was ice coursing through his body. Everything froze at the allusion to his despicable past. The memories of the cold, hard handcuffs, the bars that held him in his cage like he was a rodent… Russell had labored breathing at the mental image and the fact that Paul even knew at all!

"H-how…" Russell began. But instead of verifying Paul's knowledge, Russell decided against asking how he knew. "How…gullible do you think the judges are? I don't even know what you're talking about."

Paul ignored him.

"Maybe you should withdraw. If you do, I won't say anything," said Paul into Russell's ear. After making eye contact, he sauntered off to go check in with the judges.

Russell came back to the present. Wildly glancing around the building, Russell saw Kayla and Alexis faces as they walked away to take their seats. Their faces were lit with hope and excitement.

*Is this guy all talk? Please, God…don't let him do anything stupid. Don't let it matter…*Russell hoped his years in prison were enough atonement for the stupidity of his desperate decision. God only knew how much time he slaughtered himself for it over the years. All he wanted at this point, win or not, was to be there physically, emotionally, and financially for his girls. He hoped he wouldn't be denied that opportunity ever again.

Right before the head judge announced the competition would start and he would set the timer, Paul raised his hand from his cooking station. "I must speak with the judges privately," he declared.

Russell looked at Paul's face. It was difficult to read, devoid of any sign of pleasure or wickedness. As the judges motioned for him to walk over, he marched over with purpose. Now all Russell could do was wait to hear his fate. His head swam. He was certain the audience could see his discomfort; the guilt was clear on his face. His chest felt uncomfortably warm as it constricted; he worried he would have an asthma attack.

Paul's request halted the competition, and the audience was getting jittery. Their murmurs echoed throughout the room. Russell locked eyes with Kayla, who raised her eyebrows as if to say, "Let's hope we get this show on the road sometime before Alexis graduates!"

Russell nervously glanced over. Paul approached the head judge and whispered in his ears. Their lips tightened.

Oh, no.

They pushed their chairs away from the table and stood up.

"We apologize for the delay, but the judges are calling a brief meeting." The speaker resounded through the auditorium. Russell felt like the message was being drilled into his gut.

Please don't let my work be for nothing, thought Russell. He pled for divine help, his begging repeating and circling in his mind.

After minutes that dragged by like hours, the judges returned. Russell's heart pounded, but no one walked over to him. Paul walked to his station, appearing unphased.

Apparently, Paul's complaint about Russell's past criminal record was determined irrelevant to the competition and the judges dismissed it. The loud speaker came back on, announcing the start of the competition.

With that, he let out a huge sigh. He wasn't disqualified. He was on.

When the judge announced the time to start, Russell's mind was out of focus. Since he would only have a set time to complete his dish with the required ingredients and criteria, he needed to bring back every bit of his concentration soon. Still, though, his nerves presented itself in the new context.

"Contestants, begin!" the loudspeaker boomed. The giant analog clock started.

Standing at his cooking station, Russell felt his chest constricting. Even though he was once a water polo player, it was different in the midst of a fast-paced game. Everything in the game was straightforward: score points. Throw the ball over the opponent's net. Cooking was subjective, though. As with any art, it was difficult to know when to put it aside and feel comfortable. He had to breathe and go with his gut. He remembered telling Kayla, "Just don't think too much about measurements and what goes with what. Turn off your mind and go with your feelings."

Somehow, he did just that. He eyed the pouch of saffron and the selection of verdant vegetables in front of him before he was off. Unstoppable, Russell poured every fiber of his being into the meal. He was able to complete his dish within the limited time for the competition, even with time to spare.

To alleviate his nerves, Russell obsessively moved the sprig of parsley to the left of the plate and unfolded each leaf. He added another drizzle of orange sauce to make the zigzag design stylishly asymmetrical. His major pride and joy was his dish of mussels, a family favorite from his relatives near the coast. Each mussel was plump and glistening, appearing ready to snap out of the shell that could hardly contain it. The bright and creamy saffron sauce luxuriously cascaded over the neighboring pasta. As he sniffed the steaming dish, he could almost taste the piquant herbs.

The clock buzzed. "Time is up!"

Russell was hardly present when the judges came to his table; the cameraman and production crew from the TV station were following closely. "This is my twist on lemon and saffron linguini with steamed mussels," he said.

They each twisted some in a fork and thoughtfully chewed for what seemed an eternity. He tried reading their faces and couldn't help but feel nervous as they opened their mouths, in the meantime, managing to squeeze in some charming smiles for the cameraman robotically.

"It's nuttier. That spice really adds a lot."

"Thank you," said Russell.

The favorable remarks continued. They made their marks on their evaluation sheets and proceeded onward, sampling Paul's ravioli with brown butter and sage. Each medallion was packed and smelled great even from where Russell stood. The judges nodded and also indicated they enjoyed his work.

If nothing else, I want to beat him, Russell thought.

After agonizingly slow minutes, the loudspeaker came on once again.

"The judging period has just ended. They are now evaluating the samples and deciding upon contest winners."

Russell held his breath. He could still see Kayla and Alexis vaguely in the audience, but more people took their seats in waiting for the response. Now the crowd was like a sea of colored dots, like when he looked at a pixilated photo on the computer. While he wanted to win to feel important again, it was mainly all for them, for the women who waited for him for seven years and welcomed him back with open arms.

To excite the TV viewers, they could text message with their cell phones to vote based upon their opinions of the food preparation on television. Granted, it was only counted as a very small portion of the overall score, but TV viewers were involved.

The static of the loudspeaker shot new adrenaline through Russell's system. The lead judge announced the winners of the contest after a long period of deliberation. They started with the third prize first.

Sung Yong Lee won third prize. Not Russell. He tensed up but also held his breath in hopes for first.

"Second prize…"

Russell kept reminding himself to breath so he wouldn't pass out.

"Angela Sanchez!"

Now it was either first or nothing. The winner of a grand prize, cash reward and endorsements. The crowd was now silent in anticipation of the winner. Russell thought his pounding heart could be heard echoing throughout the premises.

"First prize of the San Francisco National Culinary Competition…is Russell Mancini!"

The crowd roared.

Wait, what? Did I just imagine they said that?

He looked around dumbly, seeing masses of people applauding him. The judges came into view, beckoning him to come accept the award and take a picture. Russell, still dumbstruck, slowly began walking toward the center of the arena. His steps felt too heavy, mechanical, as if he wasn't really there and transcended the situation. Nothing sunk in. He was in disbelief.

When the award envelope and trophy fell into his hands, with his name glinting in the metal, his face cracked open in a smile. He saw Kayla standing up and hollering, and Alexis clapping her hands with unceasing fervor – his girls, the true reason for his success.

The flashes of the camera overwhelmed Russell. He was floating with joy. The past didn't matter. He didn't care. Nothing mattered but this reality.

After the contest, Kayla got a running start and jumped into Russell's arms. Alexis hugged them both from the side, and they opened their arms to admit her. One large three-person hug. It seemed to last forever, and the world revolved around them. Kayla looked at Russell, eyes brimming with emotion.

They were swollen with joy, positively radiating it all night. Kayla's job was stable, Russell's future as a chef was guaranteed, and Alexis would be a huge help. Best of all, there would be nothing separating them this time around. Not now, not ever.

Russell received several job offers the day after the National Competition. Discussing with Kayla thoroughly, he decided to accept the position as the Manager of Chefs in a prestigious restaurant by the bay overlooking the marina with its grandiose view. It was especially famous for the magnificent night lights view and unsurpassed gourmandism.

CHAPTER 15

THE ROUTE

Caroline, "I don't know why she's saying this, but she's no shirking flower. She's the one who pulled down her pants and straddled that copy machine to Xerox her ass—strike that—let me rephrase—Buttocks."

Ms. Yi from HR, "Her account of the event is some what different." Ms. Yi looked down to the paper and read, "In order to secure my much-needed health insurance I was required to sit on the machine till she made a hundred copies."

Caroline, "Mistake. I only wanted one, but I had drunk a half a bottle of champagne—rephrase—I had one glass of wine"

Ms. Yi from HR, "I'm sorry, Miss Channing, but we will have to terminate your employment."

Caroline, "Oh, I get it now. This is what she was aiming for. She made this whole thing up to stop me from throwing my life away here at this dead end corporation—rephrase—This wonderful up-and-coming business…"

The personal entertainment center in front of Kayla's seat was showing one of the episodes of *Two Broke Girls.* [1]

Kayla looked at Russell. He slept soundly. She pushed the control buttons to switch channels. She had watched two movies and dozed in and out of the "entertainment" provided through this "personal entertainment center" since she got on the KLM Royal Dutch Airplane. That was eight hours ago, when it took off from San Francisco International Airport. It was her first international flight and everything was a brand-new and exciting experience. She was like a kid who went to Disneyland the first time in her life.

She decided to close her eyes for few minutes. She could not help but think of Alexis. This trip was the first time she had been away from her, well, except when she was in a coma.

❦

After serious consideration, Kayla made a decision about going to Bordeaux, France, for Breeana's wedding. It was to be on the first Saturday of June. Breeana had her wedding at Stefan's hometown, instead of in Paris. In spite of how Kayla and Breeana's life paths diverting in opposing directions, they continued a solid friendship for years. Through all of Kayla's curveballs in life, Breeana always offered her honest input and love from thousands of miles away. It was time that Kayla could support her in the flesh.

"Let's go a couple days early," Russell had suggested. "That way we can enjoy it for awhile."

After Russell's big win, Kayla couldn't argue – and didn't want to. It would be the honeymoon they never had. With that, they booked the tickets early for their own private adventure.

Mrs. Mancini offered to take care of Alexis because she couldn't miss school, expecially with few more weeks of school left until she had her final exams for the school year. Blooming into a teenager, their daughter pouted at the prospect of her parents going to France without her.

"We will bring you back something," said Russell. They already had a long list anyway, comprised of his parents, Dorothy, Veronica, their niece and nephew.

Never having been out of the country, Kayla couldn't believe it was reality until she hugged her daughter good-bye before they left for the airport. Alexis crossed her long arms and fake-pouted.

"You'll get your chance one day, too," said Kayla. "Now no parties while we're gone!"

Kayla heard the flight attendant gently ask her, "Madame, tea or coffee?" She realized that she had fallen asleep. Then she heard the captain's voice over the speaker.

"Ladies and Gentlemen, we are flying over Iceland and are three hours away from our destination, Schiphol International Airport in Amsterdam. The estimated landing time is 9:15 a.m. local time. Currently, we are 35,000 feet above the sea level…We will be serving breakfast shortly…"

They landed at Amsterdam-Schiphol Airport at 9:12 a.m. local time. The E-ticket showed that the next flight from there to Bordeaux departed at 10:15 a.m.—only one hour of layover time! They literally dragged their carry-on and ran from one end of the airport to the other end of the terminal. Kayla glanced at all the fancy, world-famous brands gorgeously displayed; she could not stop. They had to go through all of the inspections again before getting on board. By the time they settled down into their seats for the next flight, they both huffed and puffed. They looked at each other and laughed out loud.

Russell said, "Wow! That's cutting it too close. Now, we know. Next time, we definitely need a much longer layover time!"

"Hey, that was a good exercise after sitting on the plane for eleven and a half hours. It gave my legs some good blood circulation," replied Kayla.

They were on a smaller plane and the length of their flight was one hour and twenty-three minutes. Flying into the city, Kayla was thankful that Russell graciously gave her the window seat. Staring through the little round window (and arching her neck to see past the wing, unceremoniously obscuring her view), the first sights of France appeared to her.

"Oh, Russ." She breathed. They didn't know it was possible to fall in love at first sight, even with each other, but they were senselessly, immediately in love with Bordeaux.

They landed at Merignac Airport in Bordeaux at 12:05 p.m. local time. By the time they went through customs and claimed their luggage, it passed 1:00 p.m.

"Kayla, stay there, let me take a picture with that as a background." Right outside of the airport on the glass window, there was a big poster of two big wine glasses, one filled with white wine and the other filled with red wine. There were words "WELCOME from the Wines of Bordeaux" on top. They looked so inviting.

"Wow, we are certainly in wine country," Kayla said.

When they got in the taxi, Kayla handed the piece of paper with the hotel's name on it to the driver. The taxi driver was a friendly middle-aged man. He said in accented English, "American?" He pulled his iPhone out and spoke in French to his iPhone. Instantly the iPhone translated into English, "I just took a couple to that hotel yesterday."

Russell said to the driver's iPhone in English, "How far away from here?" The iPhone translated. "About eleven kilometers, twenty minutes." Next, the driver said, "That hotel is very close to the shopping mall and the big church."

The conversation went back and forth with iPhone as a translator. Kayla was totally amazed what the modern technology could do. She looked outside the window. There was not much traffic at that time of the day. They passed some areas that appeared to be vineyards.

"What a peaceful place! I can understand why Breeana wanted to have her wedding here."

The hotel had contemporary décor, not fancy but very clean and trendy. The lobby was on the second floor (*"the premier etage"*). There was a nice terrace and adjacent garden. They had a simple lunch at the hotel restaurant. Before returning to their room, they stopped by the lobby to ask for the city map and touring advice. Russell asked many questions about the route to the river; he had studied the map and memorized the route but wanted to confirm it again. The hotel staff was very patient and friendly with him.

"Kayla, just stand there."

Kayla was standing by one of the huge columns in front of Hotel DeVille, which also served as City Hall. There were two statues of Greek goddesses on each side of the gate. Kayla smiled and positioned herself; she appeared so small compared to the Statue. Russell tried to take pictures from different angles and distances. Their adventure had just started, but Kayla could not resist coffee from the small café in front of the DeVille Hotel.

"Wow! This is like an espresso-shot sized mug." They were sitting at the food court, sipping the coffee, seeing the boys skateboarding at the square, admiring the astounding view of St. Andre Cathedral. The surrounding was so spectacular yet tranquil.

"It seems like we have been in two different worlds within the last twenty-four hours." Kayla stared at the two sky-piercing towers of the cathedral and the bell tower (Tour Pey-Berland) nearby it.

"Do you know this cathedral has been here for over 900 years since the French started constructing the building? In 1137, the future King Louis VII married Eleanor of Aquitaine here. The exterior wall of the nave dates back to 1096."

Kayla tilted her head and looked at Russell, softly purring out an amazing sound. "Wow…"

"I looked it up online." Russell said.

"It's about time to get inside! Let's go."

They were awed by the spiritual atmosphere once they stepped inside. Russell whispered at Kayla, "When I was a little boy, I used to go with my mother to the church. She would light a prayer candle. I am going to put some money on the tray and light a candle if you don't mind."

Kayla did not quite understand the concept of "lighting a prayer candle," but Russell was so serious and sincere about it. Kayla recognized that it must have been something significant for him to do at this moment. After that, they strolled through the chapels and saw some paintings and tombs from centuries ago. The circular room of exquisite stained glass reflected variegated shapes on the ornate architecture inside. They both stared above them at the arched ceilings that echoed ages past. They were especially impressed by the huge organ. It was a spiritual and pleasant walk inside the cathedral.

As they stepped outside, Kayla studied the gigantic door frame which was lined with the fine carvings of figures. Kayla thought, *If they could talk, I would love to chat with them over a glass of wine. How do they think about the overall changes and evolution of the human race over the last 900 years? Are they disappointed in or approving of all the so called Humanity Movements?*

Russell took some pictures while Kayla was standing by the door.

"I am so wrapped up by the rich history and arts of this city, and we are only here for a few hours," Kayla said mournfully.

"Let's walk down the street." Russell urged. The street was lined up with eighteenth-century architecture. The ground level contained stores for retail or business, and the upper floors were primarily apartments. The pavement was man-laid centuries ago for horses and carriages.

Kayla remembered Breeana's advice from her last email: 1. Watch out for the pickpockets; 2. Get something you like at Bordeaux, it is as fashionable as Paris, but less expensive; and 3. Do not constantly convert euros to US dollars because it will ruin your day. Kayla held her bag in front of her. She did find a couple of blouses in a small shop and made effort not to convert euros into dollars—she really wanted to enjoy this trip!

Russell could not stop taking photos while walking down the street. "Do you remember our first date on the boat? We were making fun of those tourists taking photos nonstop? Now you're turning into one of them," Kayla joked at Russell.

"But I want to capture every moment of this day. I know my brain cannot retain all these precious moments. I need the help from this small box." He waved his camera defensively.

"But your magic box can run out of juice! This is our first day here." Kayla said.

"Don't worry. I have prepared extra batteries and memory cards. Much more than we really need. I'd rather take more photos than less. Also, I have brought my old camera as a spare. Besides, we want to show all these to Alexis, right?"

At the end of the street, they saw a post with four signs from top to bottom, all pointing to the same direction, "Grand Theatre," "La Bourse", "Place des Quinconces", and "Musee des Douanes." Another post had a bigger sign, "Porte Cailhau."

Kayla stood between two posts and was amazed by the structure in front of her. She could not help but pull her cell phone out to snap a few photos. "I will post them on my Facebook when I get back home. It makes me feel like I'm in a fairy tale, like in *Cinderella* or *Beauty and the Beast*," Kayla said.

"Oh, this gate was built in 1494, during medieval times. It was one of the main entries to the city then," Russell said and added, "I looked it up online!" Kayla let out another admiring "ooh" and "ahh."

They lingered around the gate for a while. Russell took photos from different angles and distances. Luckily, people around him were doing exactly the same thing, so he didn't look as weird as Kayla teased he would.

They walked further down and saw a big boulevard. There were some restaurants and shops along it.

"I can start to feel my legs now," Kayla said. Russell understood what she meant and said, "Let's find a place to eat and take a rest. It's almost 7 o'clock. Well, it is 10 o'clock in the morning back home! We have walked all night in California time! Where have we gotten all the energy?"

The restaurant was custom serving the tourists; the waiter gave them a menu with English translations. After studying the menu, they ordered:

Starter: *Chilled king prawns in a creamy crab sauce* for
  Kayla
Foie Gras Confit, served with asparagus and toasted
  brioche for Russell
Main course: *Poached sea bass in truffle sauce* for Kayla
Grenadine of grilled veal in Perigueux Sauce for Russell.
They shared one order of dessert: "*Fresh strawberries
  and strawberry sorbet in a strawberry coulis*"
They also ordered a bottle of local red wine: *Saint-
  Estephe* to go with their dinner.[2]

They took their time to savor the food. Kayla had to remind Russell, "Do not analyze how the chef prepared the food and the ingredients in the sauces. Just enjoy it!"

Well, it was easy to say but not easy to do. It was in Russell's genes!

It was almost 9 p.m. local time when they stepped outside the restaurant. Kayla was surprised that it was still bright outside. Russell said, "The sunset is 9:42 this evening."

"I looked it up online," Russell added mindfully.

They crossed the street to view the Garonne River. There was still one boat rolling by. They were holding hands as they slowly strolled along the sidewalk of the river, lined with trees. The sky was gradually changing color that was reflected on the water along with the bridge.

Russell recited in a low voice, "That is Pont De Pierre bridge. It was planned and commissioned by Napoleon Bonaparte when he was the first French Emperor. Look, it has seventeen arches; it echoes the seventeen letters of his name. Do you also see the medallions on the side? They were supposed to honor him."

"Russell, I am totally amazed by you! How do you know so much of French History?" Kayla could not hold back her admiration.

Then, they faced each other and said, "I looked it up online!" simultaneously.

"You know it!" Russell quietly said. He paused. "Kayla, I hope that was not the only thing that moved you this evening." He looked intensely into Kayla's eyes.

"What do you mean?

Russell gave his boyish, cavalier grin that Kayla fondly remembered from their teenage years. He shimmied away from Kayla to turn and look at her. "I'll show you how," he said. With that he straightened up before getting on one knee. He dug into his pockets, causing Kayla's heart to stop.

He can't propose, we're married...

"I know what you're thinking," he said. "We're married. But *au contraire, mon cher.* I'll show you how it's done."

He extracted a little black box from out of his pocket and slowly opened it. There sat a ring – an actual diamond ring. Kayla hadn't allowed herself to dream about such an acquisition since high school. Yet there it was, perfect, part of the dazzling scene before them. It was a fat cushion-cut diamond with a rose-gold band, and it was hers.

"Go on," Russell said. With a hesitant reach, Kayla gently touched then pressed her index finger against the stone. It was real, all right. Next Russell took it out and slid it on her finger.

Kayla could barely respond. "I…I'm trying to comprehend that this is reality," she said, smiling sheepishly. "And I don't want to do the typical cry."

Russell laughed. "Do it. You deserve a huge cry." He drew her into his arms as they both looked at her finger, now aglow with sparkles.

"Thank you," she whispered. Processing what had just occurred, Kayla pressed her face against his chest and tried to make sense of all the emotions – but thankfully, they were all good. They were so good, in fact, that she didn't know how to express them. The gratitude, relief, ecstasy, and sense of overwhelming love washed over her at once. So that's what she did: she cried, but she also laughed at the same time. After all, wasn't that their life the past few years? Wrought with tears, but held together through their conscious efforts to laugh and be positive? He gently lifted her chin up and pressed his lips against hers. They kissed deeply and passionately. Their emotions burst and merged.

With the shapes of the historical structures and cathedrals around them, the sky had turned into rich deep purplish hue. These lines resonated: [3]

> "From sullen earth, sings hymns at heaven's gate;
> For thy sweet love rememb'red such wealth brings,
> That then I scorn to change my state with kings."

Two days later, that Saturday night, Breeana was married. She was a striking goddess in Paris chiffon that floated around her in the breeze. Kayla gripped the bouquet and tried not to let the tears flow, which would inevitably mean raccoon eyes from the three layers of mascara. The entire night was a blur, as they say weddings usually are. What she did remember clear as crystal, however, were Breeana's vows. It was typical Breeana style – she had written it herself and incorporated some of Shakespeare's lines.

> "I promise to love you through the calm waters of happiness and the turbulent waves that seek to trouble our paths. Nothing will deter me, for 'Doubt that the stars are fire, Doubt that the sun doth move his aides, Doubt truth to be a liar, But never doubt I love.'" [4]

ENDNOTES

1. TWO BROKE GIRLS: season 2, episode 19, "And The Temporary Distraction."
2. Bateaux Parisiens. Menu-Spring/Summer 2011
3. William Shakespeare. Sonnet 29.
4. William Shakespeare. Hamlet, Act 2, Scene 2.